Beyond the Shadow

Julee Baker

Copyright © 2017 by Julee Baker

All rights reserved. No part of this publication may be reproduced, distributed or transmitted in any form or by any means, without prior written permission.

Publisher's Note: This is a work of fiction. Names, characters, places, and incidents are a product of the author's imagination or used fictitiously. Locales and public names are sometimes used for atmospheric purposes. Any resemblance to actual people, living or dead, or to businesses, companies, events, institutions, or locales is completely coincidental.

Publisher: Prairie Night Press

Beyond the Shadow / Julee Baker. -- 1st ed.
ISBN 978-0-9987422-0-5

For Michael

*Some heroes wear capes,
some heroes bring you coffee—lots of coffee.*
J.B.

ACKNOWLEDGEMENTS

A world of thanks to my beta readers extraordinaire, former library cohorts and enthusiasts of all things novel: Linda, Marty, Nancy, Angie, Amy, Deb, Sue, and Beth. I'm so fortunate to benefit from such a savvy group of enthusiastic readers. Your time, input, and encouragement is so appreciated.

A must mention also, are the writers I've become acquainted with, local and online. It's great to have community and share our experiences.

Special thanks to my husband, daughters, sons-in-law, and friends who have encouraged me along the way—you make the journey a joy.

Recognition to those people, from the past—such as George Bird Grinnell, instrumental in the establishment of Glacier National Park—and from the present—who work diligently to keep the wild, wondrous places the Creator has provided, protected. To those who put their lives on the line to keep us safe while we wander in, and wonder at, those places--bless you in your efforts.

CONTENTS

Wolf 1

Escape 13

Hit & Run 27

Bitter Taste 53

Cooler Meltdown 65

Photo Frame 93

Art Lesson 117

It's All Coming Back 127

Private Lessons 147

Insights Outside 171

A Visitor 185

A Hawk Grounded 203

The New Ranch Hands 219

Be Mine 239

Into the Light 257

ONE

Wolf

"**O**N YOUR WAY to grandmother's house?" The sarcasm of the man towering over photographer Lake McDonald came through loud and clear—even over the howling Montana snow squall. It chilled her more than the frigid stream she'd slipped into.

Lake tried again to gain her footing on the icy rocks, only to be pushed off balance by the intense wind. The stream was shallow, but the current could have knocked a person off balance on a good-weather day. She lifted a hand in the man's direction. At this point, wherever the guy came from, she'd be thankful for his help—even if it came with a snarky attitude.

Ignoring her dripping, finger-less gloved hand, he grabbed her upper arm and fished her from the stream in one unceremonious, but impressive move.

Feet on solid ground, Lake bent over for a moment to catch her breath, then, righted herself. She shoved the hood of her soggy red jacket back from her forehead to get a better look at her rescuer—and was surprised by the effort it took to look away from the hooded amber eyes assessing her.

She forced her focus back to the reason for her predicament—the wolf that had been chasing her down the western slope of Shadow Mountain.

Had she finally shaken it? A quick search of the tree line sent her spirit plummeting. The wolf was loping in their direction. With a startled jump, Lake grabbed the solid bicep next to her and pointed to the advancing wolf.

Her warning, "Wolf!" whooshed out in a frosty cloud, immediately carried away by the wind. His answer was a curious expression landing somewhere between a frown and a smirk.

What was wrong with him? What part of *"Wolf!"* did he *not* understand? They should get moving.

The predator's nearness trigged Lake's flight response. Her feet were moving—but in a Fred Flintstone like motion that was getting her nowhere. Alarmed by the iron grip holding her in place, she pulled harder, in a futile attempt to free herself.

Over the broad shoulder, she could see the animal—now less than ten feet away—where it stopped, then proceeded to vigorously shake the snow from its coat and—wag its tail? Its hearty "Wooo-ooof" sounded more like a laugh than a threat.

What the—? Lake's frozen brows scrunched together—then went pink—along with the rest of her. The "big, bad wolf" she'd been eluding the past half an hour—was evidently some kind of Malamute or Husky, mixed-breed dog. But, seriously—how could she have known? In this storm—covered with snow—well, the dog had looked very wolfish indeed.

"Your d-dog?" She leaned closer to the man to be heard over the wind, attempting a smile, but another gust of icy crystals blasted across her face, drawing a wince instead.

"Yeah." His answer was curt and delivered as he looked her over from top to—well, all-over.

A blush of warmth pulsed through Lake at the inspection. At least her body could still produce heat. A shaky laugh slipped through her chattering teeth. "I-I th-though it w-was a w-wolf."

He shook his head. And . . . was that an eye-roll? Then, almost inaudible, came the low grumble, "Classic newbie."

"Whoa . . . Wait a . . ." Did he just call her a newbie? "I'm no newbie." Lake turned up the volume on her denial—although realizing the present situation did little to support her claim.

Any leftover warmth from her blush of embarrassment had lingered no more than a nanosecond—now replaced by a bone-shaking shiver. Man, she hadn't felt this kind of cold before—not even on those nights up near Anchorage, when she and her parents had photographed that gorgeous series of aurora.

The thought pierced like a knife—the late summer plane crash that took them—still too fresh. She forced her focus back to the man staring at her. Under the stocking cap and gray hoodie—a fierce scowl now etched his dark brow.

His voice was gruff and contained a note of urgency. "You're ten minutes away from turning into a human popsicle. We need to get you warm—fast."

Warmth—she couldn't agree more. "Right. My Jeep's over . . . a . . . it's right over—" The wind threatened to eat her words as she turned three-quarters of a circle, shouting, "there . . . I'm pretty sure."

Aggravation? Lake watched the amber eyes flash hot. Not a *wow*-hot . . . well, okay, even in her half-frozen state she had to admit they were . . . but something else . . . an *angry* hot.

"Pretty sure will get you pretty dead, pretty quick out here," he shouted back at her and nodded in the direction she'd pointed. "There's nothing that that way but billions of tons of granite we like to call the *Rockies*."

After a look up the mountain, he turned back to her. A couple days of dark growth scraped across her cheek as he leaned to her ear with a curt command, "Follow me. This could get worse. My cabin's nearby. You need to get dry."

He turned and started back up the slope.

"I can't." She hollered at the broad back.

He turned back, concern sounding in his question, "Can't walk?"

She shook her head. "No. Of course I can walk. But my camera..."

Lake opened her mouth to say more, but shut it and winced as another gust of frozen bee bees hit her face. After the blast passed, she continued, "I dropped my camera back there. I need to find it."

That was an understatement—she needed that camera in the worst way. At least now, she'd have his help. Which way? Her eyes searched the wall of white behind her. Earlier in the day she'd gotten several spectacular shots. The final draft was due soon, finding that camera was crucial. If she could just manage to finish the book her parents had been working on—well, it could help her and River dig out of the financial hole their parents' deaths had left them in. Plus, there was no way she could afford to replace that camera right now. It was her star piece of equipment—her and River's livelihood.

"No way—not today."

"You don't understand," she motioned with her arms... then frowned. What was the matter with her arms? They moved in slow motion. Weird...

"No. C'mon." He walked away from her.

"But, I need—"

"No," came the stern command.

He didn't even turn around for the last one.

Unreasonable... Arrgh... She had no choice. All she could do was hope the waterproof case lived up to its price tag. With a sigh and a last look behind her, Lake gave up and trudged after the abominable *"No!"* man in front of her, his form now fading into the billowing white that lay ahead.

Could nothing go right anymore?

Back in the day, in the safe little universe where she used to live, she would have prayed. Back in the day, she believed God listened. Back in the day, she would have cried. Back in the day—before she'd cried herself empty—before God forgot about the McDonalds.

Lake shook the thoughts off and struggled after the man and dog. Her wet jeans were stiffening in the freezing temps. Her legs felt like lead . . . what she could still feel of them. And her hands—those fingerless gloves were great for working the camera and changing lenses—not so much when it came to keeping hands warm in blizzards.

A couple hundred stumbling feet later, she had to stop and rest for a moment—close her eyes from the biting wind. When she opened them, the man was back in front of her. He was talking. Huh. She watched with a detached fascination as he took his own stocking cap off and pulled it over her head, then pulled his sweatshirt hood up over his own dark hair, which had quickly been dusted with frozen bits. He then turned his attention to her hands as another violent shiver shook her. He peeled off her wet half-gloves and discarded them.

If she lived to be a hundred, she would never forget the transfusion of warmth when the strong, tanned hands closed over hers. He slipped his too-large, but oh-so-warm gloves over her hands. Lake sent a silent glance of appreciation to the dark-fringed, amber eyes.

The wind around them howled like a beast ready to feed. She realized he was saying something to her. Lake struggled to hear.

"Get on my back." He motioned to his back.

"What?"

"Piggyback. You'll never get up there at this rate. You need to get warm. Hurry up."

She felt so tired—and confused. "You don't understand. My camera—I need to find it."

A grumble rumbled from deep in the broad chest, right before he pulled her on like a backpack and set off. She couldn't have matched his pace under ideal conditions.

Shivers became shudders. Lake gave up. All she could do was cling to him—this rock of a man. Her former boyfriend, Jeremy, was no wimp—well not physically anyway—but no match for this guy. Burrowing her head against his shoulder, she concentrated on holding on.

Lake felt almost one with him as he worked his way up the rough trail. It was a weird feeling, relying on someone else again. It seemed a lifetime ago since she'd felt that luxury. His muscles worked a steady rhythm, his strength evident even through the heavy clothing. Cold as she was, an unexpected moment of contentment stole over her.

Thank G . . . She stopped herself. Huh, old habits . . . old useless habits . . .

Every once in a while, a heavy breath or grunt sounded over the wind as he struggled up the steep terrain. With his arms holding her legs around his sides, it had to affect his ability to balance, but there was no stopping him from his mission. Stamina like this took serious training. Ex-military? Such determination.

A punishing gust sucked away another frosty breath. She burrowed her face tighter. What a mess. What would her parents have thought? She'd rushed preparations—that's what. Always risky—bad mistake. But she needed to finish their book in the worst way. All those funeral expenses . . . then the bills . . . and all their parents' money tied up in a piece of property they'd planned to build their dream home on. Next to nothing was left on hand.

And now, her best camera was MIA—boomeranged away when a stray branch caught the strap during her run from the wolf. The perfect photos were on that camera, along with spectacular *Snowshine on Shadow* shots. Incredible shots. She could have worked those into a future exhibit.

Current financial worries had clouded her judgment in her rush to prepare. She couldn't afford to make mistakes. Blunders like this weren't only hers now. Six-year-old River, was the only family she had left. She couldn't, *wouldn't* let her little brother down.

Lake's eyes, squinted shut against the biting cold, opened at the solid thump of boots on wooden porch steps. She was peeled off her rescuer's back—peeled because she couldn't seem to move herself. Brain told body to move, but body ignored. He set her on her feet with a loud clunk at the cabin door, his arm still supporting.

His dark beard stubble scraped her cheek again and she caught a warm, woodsy scent as he leaned toward her ear.

"It'll take a few minutes to get your land legs back." He brushed snow from her and then himself.

No kidding. Lake studied him.

Out of the wind and with no need to shout, his voice had a pleasant, husky timbre a person might even call magnetic. The kind of voice people paid attention to. Lake forced her stare down to her legs and rubbed at them. Still numbed from cold, they wouldn't obey.

Observing her trouble, he picked her up and pushed the door open with his foot. The big dog budged ahead and ran toward the hearth as they entered his cabin . . . if you could call a structure this beautiful a cabin. Lake blinked her surprise. More like a ski resort. Not huge, but spacious. Glowing firelight danced and shimmered over golden woods from floor to beamed cathedral ceilings and walls of glass. Stunning.

The welcoming warmth of the wood fire enfolded her. Warmth . . . ohhh. Had anything ever felt as wonderful?

"Sit next to Elle. I'll try to find something dry that you can wear."

"Oooow wooooorrr."

Lake jumped at the dog's comment.

"A wolf? Comical. Elle wouldn't hurt a mouse." He turned to the dog. "You behave yourself."

After another sassy, "Wooo-oo-ooo," Elle laid her head across Lake's thigh.

"Yeah, don't get too attached to our visitor, Elle. What we've got here, I believe, is one of Colter's spies, snooping around the old mine . . . again. I should knock the guy from here to Kalispell for sending a greenhorn out here on a day like this." The low muttering continued as he worked his boots off.

Lake frowned. "Snooping? What? I—I have no idea what you're talking about. Listen—my name's Lake McDonald. I'm a photographer. I have permission from the Conservancy to photograph on Shadow. I have a release form." Lake's cold fingers fumbled through her pockets. "It must have fallen out of my pocket, but I can assure you . . ."

She stopped at his look. Sure, a lot of people were confused by her name—it sounded more like a place than a woman's name—but this guy looked—almost stunned.

"Lake . . . McDonald," he repeated softly.

She smiled at him and shook her head, squeezing water from the dark-brown, side-braid she always wore. "I know, I know. Lake McDonald . . . that's a place, not a name, right? My parents fell in love with the lake in Glacier Park." She renewed her smile and continued, "With the last name McDonald, well, I guess they couldn't resist. I get it all the time. I'm used to—"

A buzz and crackle pulled both their attention to a shortwave radio sparking to life on a corner table.

"Aidan . . . Matthews . . . Matthews come in . . . Hawk . . . Hawk . . . you there? It's Sam. We've got a missing woman. It's . . ."

Lake couldn't hear the rest. With three long strides, Aidan "Hawk" Matthews had moved to the radio and grabbed the headset. "She's here Sam . . . Cold, but okay. Yeah. Uh-huh. Umm . . . don't know yet." He signed off, but hesitated before turning back to Lake in grim silence.

Lake's expression turned from stunned to stone. Aidan "Hawk" Matthews. She knew that name . . . in her darkest moments—had cursed that name.

Lake stood to face the man responsible for her parents' deaths.

TWO

Escape

"You," she choked. Her knees trembled. Any heat from the massive stone fireplace was snuffed by the chill that fell over the room.

"Yeah . . . me." Hawk Matthews locked her in a look that took them both right back to the night of her parents' plane crash. Only this time, there was no crackling phone line, no blizzard, no half-continent between them.

Her hand fisted. Thoughts of pleading with him the night of the crash came back as vividly as if they had happened yesterday. There had been no getting through to the unfeeling monster—it was this man's decision that had called off the search that night—dooming her parents. She wanted to smack his arrogant jaw.

Little good it would do; her fist would bounce off him like a tennis ball off a brick wall. Lake forced herself back to calm—an outward calm anyway. Hadn't she preached to River—physical violence doesn't solve anything?

Matthews had noticed her hand clench.

"You gonna hit me?" A dark brow raised.

Lake seethed. Better to get out of there and away from this . . . this . . . Her jeep couldn't be that far—just a matter of following the drive to the main road. She turned toward the door, but the six-foot something wall of him blocked the way.

"Don't even think about it. You'd freeze to death."

"Like my parents did?" Lake snapped. Well, well—that drew a wince. Did he have any remorse? Any realization of how much devastation his mistake had caused?

"Get out of my way."

He didn't move.

"Listen." He rubbed his jaw, considering her. "We should talk. I know what you think of me. Believe me, I've heard it around town . . . but, right now, you need to get dry. Sit by the fire. Let me get those towels and dry clothes."

Lake wanted none of it, but couldn't very well pick him up and move him out of the way, so she conceded—for the moment. Her mind whirring to figure out an escape, she sat down by the fire, next to the dog.

With her move back to the hearth, Hawk Matthews unlaced and pulled off his boots, then headed toward the back of the cabin. "Take your boots off. Like it or not, you're stuck here for a while."

Don't bet on it. Lake thought the words loudly. She could have sworn he heard them when he shot her a dark look, then disappeared down the hall.

Stuck here? Forget that. Fate worse than death. The late afternoon light was fading fast. Situated between mountains, twilight—what there was of it—lasted only a few minutes. Lake squinted at the view out the expansive windows. The snow hadn't stopped, but it had let up considerably, now falling in a soft Christmas card vertical, instead of the blinding horizontal of earlier.

It was then she spotted it. A truck—a silver four by four—parked in front of the cabin. A plan bloomed. This could be her ticket out. A lot of people out on these ranches left the keys in everything. If Matthews followed the local norm, she could use the truck to get to her jeep. It couldn't be more than a quarter mile or so. Then, she could get home . . . home to River and out of this *Hitchockian* nightmare.

The fire had revived Lake, but the anger roiling within her set her on fire. With hearing tuned to the noise of drawers opening and closing in the back rooms, she pulled her wet boots back on over her wet socks and sneaked to the front door. It was a testament to the builders that the golden pine floors didn't make one squeak as she stole across them.

Well, he was right about one thing. Her chances of walking back to her jeep in this weather—not good. Huh—Matthews should know about freezing—he'd condemned her parents to it.

Stop it Lake. Don't think about it now. She forced her mind back to the present. Get to the truck, drive to the jeep.

Lake opened the door, but not before pulling off Matthews's stocking hat and throwing it to the floor in disgust. She opened the door and slipped outside—which set off a barkfest from the dog.

The dog. She hadn't considered the dog. The commotion sent her in a slippery sprint to the truck.

She slipped and slid across the yard, slamming into the driver's door. Unlocked. Her eyes darted to the steering column. Keys. *Yes.*

She swung in and started the engine just as Matthews came charging out the front door, hopping and pulling on a boot, the barking dog close behind. It gave Lake a new visual to associate with the term—hopping mad. Satisfaction at putting that expression on his face gave her a charge of adrenaline. She stomped the gas pedal and sent the truck in a fishtail away from the cabin, the vision of an angry Hawk Matthews and his dog receding quickly in the rearview mirror.

"Whoooooa!" The truck skidded around the first curve sobering her to a rational speed. The road was slick and covered with small drifts. Her heart threatened to beat through her chest. Deep breaths. Calm down. She was losing daylight, but the last thing she needed was to send Matthews's truck—and herself—down the side of the mountain.

Thankfully, the snow had all but stopped. Good thing the truck was four-wheel drive. Pretty much mandatory around here.

It was slow going with the edge of the road barely visible. After only a couple minutes of white-knuckle driving, her jeep came into view. It was at the side of the road—surrounded by a foot and a half drift.

You've got to be kidding.

The wind had packed the snow against, around, and under the jeep. Efforts to drive out only left it high-centered. Four-wheel drives were great, but not invincible.

Chilled to the bone, with spirits sinking, Lake looked around. The light was almost gone. She needed to get home to River before dark . . . and get as far away from Matthews as she could.

Only one option seemed available.

Desperate times—desperate measures and all that. She'd *borrow* the truck a little longer and get it back to him tomorrow, somehow. A stop at Sheriff Patrick's in the morning was a definite priority, too. Early. It had been Sam Patrick's voice on the shortwave. Fran must have called him.

In her frenzy to get away from Matthews, Lake hadn't spent much time considering the consequences of her—borrowing—plan until now. She sure hoped Sam saw the difference between borrowing and grand theft auto the same way she did. Her gaze swept the road behind, half expecting Matthews to appear out of the dusk.

Twenty minutes later, a relieved Lake pried ice-cold fingers from the steering wheel and trudged up the stairs to her apartment over the studio. What a day—what luck—running into the man she would least want to run into in the entire world—let alone be obligated to in any way.

Now that she was safe, exhaustion and near hypothermia, hit like a freight train. Fran's anxious face greeted her from the window. She practically bowled Lake over at the door.

"Oh. Thank the Lord you're home. You had me so worried. I called the sheriff's office," she added in a whisper, glancing toward River's room. Then, looking back out the window, "Is that Hawk's truck? Is he outside? Where's your Jeep?"

"You know Matthews?" Lake was taken aback.

"A little. Pretty much everyone knows Hawk around here."

"I've been here all winter. How come I've never seen him?"

"He's been on the news."

"I guess I haven't watched the news much since—" Lake stopped.

Her parents' plane crash had been reported incessantly at first, and even now, random reports popped up for one reason or another. The therapist said children are resilient, but, every plane crash reported on TV triggered stress for River. It had been easier to avoid the news altogether—for his sake—or was it for hers?

Fran seemed to catch her train of thought and hurried past, "It's been a hard winter, Lake. Slowed us all down." Placing a gentle hand on Lake's shoulder, she said, "Now that spring is here, it'll get better. And, I'm sure we'll all be getting reacquainted."

Lake's tone was flat. "You forget, Matthews was responsible for postponing the search for Mom and Dad. I talked to him from Chicago, the night of the crash. He'd called off the search and we argued. I want nothing more to do with him. I have absolutely no desire to get reacquainted with the man who botched the search for Mom and Dad. All I want to do is get his truck back to him—A. S. A. P."

"Lake! Lake! You're home!" River burst upon the scene dressed in his PJs, plowing full force into Lake, wrapping his arms around her legs tightly. "You're late." He frowned, and backed up. "And you're all cold 'n' wet."

Lake bent over and hugged him. "I'm okay, buddy. Everything's okay. I had a little trouble with the jeep." She kissed his cheek. "Sorry it took so long. My phone wouldn't work in the mountains and with this storm."

She hugged him tighter. "Did you have a fun day with Fran?" She needed to get things back on a normal note.

"Yeah. Lots. We watched Ranger Randy and I ate oatmeal and then we drew horses, then we drew dinosaurs, then we colored cars, then we ate hot dogs. Oh! Lake. You should make these little wrapped up hot dogs Fran makes. They're pigs in blankets. Isn't that funny? They're really good and-"

"Hey, hey buddy—take a breath." Lake couldn't help but smile at River's enthusiasm. It was the only fuel able to recharge her lately. The first two months were especially rough, but since he'd discovered Ranger Randy on a local children's TV show, and with River's intense interest in animals and drawing, she'd been able to channel his attention. "But now that I'm here, we better let Fran get home and you," she tweaked his nose, "to bed." She gave him another hug and turned him toward his room. "Thank Fran and go hop in bed. I'll be there in a couple of minutes to tuck you in."

"Ooo—kay." He dragged out the word in a descending sing-song. "G'night Fran. Thank you. I had a fun day."

Fran answered River, then turned her attention to Lake, looking her over.

"Want to talk about it?"

"You would not believe the day I've had . . . I hardly believe it myself. What. A. Nightmare." She plopped down on the couch shaking her head. "I got some of the best shots ever, up on Shadow, then lost them . . . and my best camera. Then . . ." Lake pulled her wet socks off in a ball and fast-pitched them to the corner. "Then, I ran into Matthews." Lake's shoulders slumped.

Fran came over and put an arm around her. "What in the world?"

She gave Fran the short synopsis, ending with a defensive explanation of just how Hawk Matthews's truck ended up outside her apartment.

"You know, Lake, Hawk was in a tough position the night you talked to him . . ."

"You're defending him?" She didn't want to be angry with Fran, but there was no discussion on the subject. "Mom and Dad were the ones in a tough position. Those guys are supposed to be trained for extreme rescues—," she trailed off.

Fran moved the subject away from the crash—though not far enough. "Decent of him to let you borrow his truck . . . though I'm kind of surprised he didn't drive you himself." She frowned, considering.

"A . . . He didn't . . . well . . . I mean . . . didn't exactly . . . give his permission . . ."

Fran's eyebrows raised and jaw dropped at the same time. "Lake . . . what did you do?"

Lake's explanation tumbled out faster than River's had a few minutes before. "I had to get out of there. All I wanted to do was get to my jeep, but it was drifted in. I'm heading to Sam's first thing tomorrow to straighten things out." Was Fran smirking? She was a little put off by the older woman's amusement at her predicament.

"I'd like to hear about it, but you look like you're about to drop. Get into some nice warm jammies and get some sleep." She made a few shoo-ing motions, then picked up her coat and put it on. "Call me in the morning if you need bail money." Fran gave her another hug. "I'm so relieved you're home safe, hon. G'night."

With Fran's exit, Lake stripped off her wet jeans and shirt. She pulled on a dry sweatshirt, pants and socks from the purple laundry basket on the dryer and headed for River's room. Passing the couch, she decided to sit for a moment to calm her thoughts—or push thoughts—like Matthews, out of her head. Just a couple minutes . . . just to rest her eyes . . . as she . . . slowly . . . tipped . . . over . . .

***

A patient River waited for his "tuck in," but after twenty minutes, peeked out his door to see what was keeping his sister. He found her on the couch, sound asleep. Moving to the end of the couch, he pulled the double wedding ring quilt his mom had made from her mom's and grandmother's dresses over them and snuggled beside her.

"I miss mom and dad," he whispered.

Lake cuddled River closer. "I miss them too, Riv."

"'Night. Love you".

"Love you too." Lake mumbled into his dark hair and kissed the top of his head, half-conscious as she pulled the quilt up tighter around them both.

***

Hawk ended a frustrating day with another frustration when the snowmobile wouldn't start. The wrench clanked as it slammed into the other tools in the box—the victim of an uncharacteristic show of frustration.

"You've got to be kidding. That just tops—" followed by a string of words that made Myron's ears twitch. The normally calm, old stallion stomped the floor in his stall at the other end of the barn.

Hawk's intentions had been to cut the truck off with the snowmobile by crossing over a couple of foothills to the south of his place. Carrying the thought further, there probably wasn't enough time to catch her anyway. Hawk eyed the yellow dirt bike in the corner. No, too much snow.

Elle tilted her head sideways at him, the way dogs do when trying to make sense of their human. The gesture always brought a smile to Hawk's face. Well, maybe half-smile today.

"Not you, girl." He squatted down and wrapped an arm around the dog, ruffling the fur on her chest then patting her on the side. "You were great. Good dog. Very good dog." Elle responded with wagging tail and slobbery kisses.

A soft nicker, followed by a loud snort, sounded from the back of the building.

"Myron?" Hawk smiled at the old horse. "No guy, not today."

The horse stomped its foot and gave another snort.

"No way old boy. Not on a day like this."

Myron was a three-year old when Hawk's grandfather gave him the buckskin quarter horse for his fourteenth birthday. Now, eighteen years later, the sweet old horse was still rarin' to go.

He walked over and rubbed the horse's muzzle and neck. "I know you'd try if I asked you to." After another rub to the horse's neck, he went back to the snowmobile.

It was imperative he get that machine working soon. Not good to be out here without it. He mentally kicked himself for letting a crucial piece of equipment go down, too much time—in the zone—working his art and not enough in the shed working on vehicles. But the Colorado show was coming up fast. He needed to get the promised pieces done.

Hawk crossed his arms over his chest and exhaled. "No truck, a snowmobile that won't start and not enough sleep." Hawk rubbed his forehead. "McDonald . . . *Lake* McDonald . . . What are the chances?" Elle listened attentively. "You know what?" Elle's head tilted again, this time in the opposite direction, as if it might help. "Tomorrow better bring a truck sitting back in the drive or someone's going to jail for grand theft auto." Hawk ground out the threat. The threat he knew he could never carry out against her. Too much heartache of his own about the way the McDonalds' recovery had gone.

Why can't I shake it, Lord? I know You're the only miracle worker around here . . . But why . . . why couldn't I have had one—just one miracle, that night?

"Woof."

Elle's response pulled a little of his frown away. Hawk patted her side again. Like it or not, he had sympathy for Lake. "I guess I might have high-tailed it away from me too," he thought aloud. Her comments about him around town had gotten back to him—and hit him where it hurt. All he wanted to do, trained to do, was help people. In a town the size of Harmony, the grapevine wasn't long.

"Woo-oof."

"Hey. No comments. You grumbled plenty when you had to get off the couch earlier." He gave the dog a good-natured pat.

He didn't want to send anyone to jail. Well, maybe John Colter. He'd better go radio Sam to do a drive by and see if Lake McDonald and his truck made it back to town okay. The snow had tapered off about the time she left. She shouldn't experience a problem from the weather—but the emotional state she was in when she peeled out—that was another story.

"C'mon girl. I'm hungry. You hungry? Want some grub?"

Ahh . . . the magic word.

"Woo-ooo-oof."

What would he do without this dog? "Let's grab supper and call it a night. We've got a truck to track down and a whole lot to sort out tomorrow."

THREE

Hit & Run

Flllummp. Lake awoke with a start to the sound of River and the quilt slipping off the couch.

"Oh. Buddy. Are you okay?"

River giggled and stretched. "You hogged practically all the room on the couch last night."

"I'm *sooo* sorry, bud. I fell asleep before I could tuck you in."

What kind of a "mom" was she going to be if she couldn't even handle tucking-in-to-bed duties?

"That's okay. I came to see what was taking you so long and then I decided to cover you, but I was tired too, so I just snuggled up."

Lake pulled him over for a hug. "Thanks, Riv." He was the sweetest kid. He deserved the best—big sis-mom—she could be.

"C'mon tiger . . . let's eat breakfast. Then, we'll get ready for church. I'm starving."

"Me too. Can you make those mouse pancakes with the blueberry eyes?"

"Sure thing, kiddo. But it'll have to be fast. You'll have to jump into your clothes after pancakes. And be quick."

She checked her watch. Ten to eight. They should leave for church by eight forty-five.

Her struggles shouldn't keep River from attending. No matter where their parents had been working, they always attempted to find a church and Riv needed all the continuity she could provide right now. Faith, and practicing what you preach had always been important to their parents. She would make sure to honor those values for River.

But, anymore, the only prayer—if you could even call it a prayer—she could manage was, *"Why, God?"*

River ate his pancakes with gusto. While he got dressed, Lake took a speed shower. She had to address the matter of the truck as soon as possible.

She pulled the peachy towel tighter around her and walked to the window, parting the curtains slightly. The silver problem still sat in the street in front of the apartment. She'd been wishing Matthews's four-by-four would have disintegrated during the night like a bad dream. No such luck. There it sat, chrome grill grinning her direction. Sheriff Patrick would have to be called—ASAP—preferably before he came looking for her—warrant in hand.

Lake jumped into jeans and a Cubs sweatshirt. Hair still damp, she called Sam's non-emergency number.

"Sheriff's office."

Uh-oh. Sounded like he could use another cup of coffee, or two.

"Good morning, Sam. It's Lake McDonald. How are you?"

"Mornin', Lake. "How am I? Hmm—been better. Bad accident, south of town around midnight. Didn't get my beauty sleep. And earlier in the day we were quite concerned about a photographer that hadn't returned from hiking..."

"A—yes—about that—" Lake tumbled through her explanation of yesterday's events, trying to be as concise as possible, but ended up spilling words out all over each other when she came to the part about *borrowing* Matthews's truck.

***

Sam listened to Lake stammer through her explanation with concern—though not for quite the same reasons she thought important. Hawk had radioed last night alerting him to the situation, so he'd already checked out the side street where Lake normally parked and seen Hawk's truck, verifying that she'd made it back to town okay.

Hawk and Lake's meeting under yesterday's circumstances was not a welcome turn of events—seeing as how Sam had hoped the two could come to a better understanding of one another. He and Hawk had been good friends since high school sports and he hadn't mentioned to him that Lake had moved into the apartment above her folks' photography studio down the street. Sam, more than anyone, realized Hawk didn't need to be reminded of the McDonald ordeal. The guy was still beating himself up about having to postpone the search that night. His friend considered it a failure, but, as far as Sam was concerned, he'd gone above and beyond the call of duty—especially after they'd almost lost one of their own team. The blizzard was plain, old bad luck on top of bad luck.

As for Lake, Sam had enjoyed their brief meetings and wanted to get better acquainted with the pretty photographer—maybe even change her opinion about Hawk at some point.

It would take a lot of doing. That woman had a lot on her plate right now.

Sam could imagine what Hawk's attitude must have been when he found her yesterday—considering Hawk thought she was one of Colter's flunkies. With the frequency that Colter, or one of his goons had been nosing around Shadow lately, well, Sam would be willing to bet smoke was coming out of his friend's ears. Then, to find out she was Caleb and Anne McDonald's daughter...

Lake's explanation spiraled on. "—and I really couldn't stay there a moment longer. I had to get to my Jeep. Then, when I got there, it was drifted in . . . and I needed to get home to River. He's been having nightmares lately and I couldn't have him worrying. Not to mention Fran and . . ."

Okay—time to be merciful and put an end to her stumbling explanation.

"Whoa, Lake—slow down. It's okay. Taking off with his truck wasn't the best way to handle things—but, what's done is done. I mean, not everyone would be as understanding as Hawk. He radioed in last night. Wanted to make sure you got back to town. So, I've already been briefed on the whole story."

"Oh . . . well, good." A moment's pause, then, "So—I won't be arrested?"

"He's not pressing any charges. You're not going to be arrested."

The relief was evident in her voice. "It's supposed to get up to the upper fifties. The snow should melt fast. I'm thinking of driving the truck up to his place right after church this morning. I'll put the truck in his drive and walk down the road to my Jeep." she finished.

"Listen. I agree. Make getting the truck back a priority. I'll let him know you'll drive it back this morning."

"I'm relieved I won't have to take Fran up on her offer of bail money. Thanks. I owe you big time."

"You don't owe me anything. But, it does sound like you need to take a break. Let me buy you dinner at Suzanne's."

"Well . . . I don't know . . . It looks like today will be filled with shuffling vehicles around and I've got a few other things to do, but, how about tomorrow night? Suzanne's around six-thirty? River is signed up for a Young Artists class at the art center. He'll be busy making clay animals until eight-thirty, so that would work for me. How about you? But, you don't need to treat."

"I'd like to buy, but, if that's a condition . . . I'll see you then. And, take it slow driving up to Hawk's. It's melting, but it'll be slick where the sun hasn't hit the road yet."

"I'll be careful. I've had more than enough excitement this weekend."

No sooner had he ended the call with Lake, then his radio sounded—a car and a deer had tangled south of town. "Not again." With a tired grown, he grabbed his hat and headed back to the patrol car.

The call to Hawk would have to wait.

***

Church let out shortly after ten o'clock. For Lake, it had never really started. Oh, she'd been going through the motions for River's sake, but, for months now, she couldn't get her mind into the readings. A Bible reading used to be a morning ritual. It now lay in exile in the bottom drawer of her dresser.

And this morning, she had the additional distraction of how to return the 'borrowed' truck to Hawk Matthews . . . of all the people in the world . . .

River's, "Can I Lake? Can I? Can I?" pulled her attention back to the present as they exited the church into the bright sunlight. River's friend from Sunday school, Zach, invited him to spend the afternoon. Of course, she agreed. It was wonderful River had a good friend . . . and it eliminated the need to call on Fran again. No way was River coming along on the truck errand.

Lake patted her pocket again. She had checked and rechecked it to make sure she had the spare set of Jeep keys. Oh, yes . . . this could get interesting. According to Sam, Matthews wasn't a threat. Still, she didn't want any trouble. Hopefully, she could deposit the truck in his drive and be gone before he even realized she'd been there.

Yikes. She filled the tank and watched the dollar dial spin. More than he deserved. Soon, the big silver Chevy purred down the road. Today's warmer temps and bright sunshine were quickly turning winter's last blast to rivulets and large, slushy puddles. Amazing what a difference a day made.

All she wanted to do at this point, was to get the truck back to Matthews's place and wipe yesterday's episode out of her mind.

Well, except for the camera. Finding it was a problem yet to be solved.

As she neared Matthews's place, an attack of nerves caused her to review her plan. She psyched herself. Right. Okay. Get in and out fast. Leave the truck in the drive, unnoticed.

Why hadn't she asked Sam or Fran or, basically anyone else, to do this favor for her? Maybe she could have talked Suzanne from the diner into helping her out. Heaven knows, she'd bought enough gooey pecan rolls in the past five months to start a college fund for that cute little girl of hers.

Too late now. She'd managed tougher things. She straightened up. The sooner anything involving Matthews was over, the better.

There—visible just beyond the last big curve before Matthews's lane—the Jeep. A quick scan showed the drift had shrunk to half its previous size. Yes. No problem. She could drive right over what remained.

Did she dare look around for the missing camera? She needed it—those photos. They could be key to her and River's future—or would it be better to wait a day or two and try to enlist some help?

These thoughts occupying her attention, she nearly missed spotting the animal laying at the side of the road. It looked like—a dog.

Matthews's dog.

She swerved sharply to the right and parked off the road in front of the animal, dreading what she might find. As feared, it was his beautiful dog, lying motionless. Her stomach lurched as she dropped to her knees on the wet ground beside the wounded animal.

What had happened? She looked around—no one. Did someone hit the dog and leave her there? Couldn't they have stopped? Anger rose in Lake—no matter what her opinion of the dog's owner, she had to help. What was its name? She'd been so upset yesterday, she strained to remember. E something. Elle—that's what Matthews called her, wasn't it?

A slight whine.

"Elle . . . Elle . . . good girl . . . yeah." Should she touch a wounded animal? Lake gave a tentative stroke to the big dog's shoulder. "Shhh, shhh . . . I'm gonna help you . . . It's gonna be okay."

But how? Could she lift the big dog into the truck? Would it bite out of fear? From the looks of her, she must weigh—what—seventy-five pounds? She'd have to try. Who knows how long she'd been lying out here, and what kind of injuries she had. If she could get her to the vet.

"Elle . . . girl . . . it's okay . . . I'm gonna put you in the truck." After a couple of tentative touches to see how the dog would react, it seemed safe enough to try and work her arms under the dog. "It's okay . . . that a girl," reassuring the dog as she worked to lift her. She inhaled deeply. This wasn't going to be easy. At least Elle, for her part, was not resisting. Was that a good or bad sign?

Lord, please help me help her. It came out before she had time to think about it—or overrule the errant thought. She'd pretty much given up on prayer since the crash. With a frown, she refocused on the dog.

Ignoring her stinging knees, Lake worked her arms carefully under the dog, trying to figure out how to leverage standing up while holding a seventy-five-pound dog, when, around the bend buzzed a dirt bike.

Huh? . . . An answer to her prayer?

The dirt bike's spinning tires sprayed gravel her direction as its driver skidded to a stop and dropped the bike on its side, engine barely off. The rider evidently recognized the urgency of the situation.

Removal of the black helmet revealed an all too familiar face.

Matthews.

Good thing she was already kneeling, as any strength left in her legs evaporated.

"What the . . . Elle . . ." His stricken expression went from his dog, to her, and back to the dog again, as he went to his knees and began, gently and methodically, running his hands over the entire dog.

Hawk Matthews's next statement came out subdued—she supposed he didn't want to frighten the dog—but it had the menacing low rumble of a volcano about to explode.

"What'd you do? Hit my dog with my truck? I know you hate me but—" His shot a searing look her way before turning back to the dog.

"No." Lake defended herself. "No, I didn't hit your dog." No matter what she thought of him, she would never . . . could never let anyone, even him, think she would do something like . . .

A loud whimper drew their attention.

"Elle. Elle, girl . . . it'll be all right . . ." He gently lifted the side of the dog's mouth, speaking to himself as he examined. "Gums still pink—good. She's awful quiet . . . not good . . . breathing hard. She may be going into shock." He felt her stomach. "Hope her spleen's not ruptured . . . probably already be dead if it was. Side's pretty scraped up." He nodded to the four-by-four as he lifted the injured dog and ground out an order. "Get in the passenger side."

At her hesitation, he continued, "We've got to get her to the vet—now. And you're going to help me—like it or not. Move!"

No matter what she thought of him, she needed to correct his assumption that she hit the dog—but, the important mission right now was a helpless animal suffering because of an irresponsible driver's carelessness.

"I'm heading to Doc Simon's. Get in—you can hold Elle in your lap while I drive."

Lake stepped up into the passenger seat.

"Seatbelt." Matthews ordered. She tried to comply, but couldn't reach it as he laid the dog across her lap. Placing her arms around the dog, he told her, "Keep your arm across—there and the other right—here. She's heavy, but you need to hold her as still as possible," he insisted.

The amber eyes held a fiery insistence and Lake could do nothing but nod.

Pulling a backpack from behind the seat, he propped it under the dog's head, then, removing his leather jacket, he placed it over them. As she held the dog, he reached past and grabbed the seatbelt, fastening it around her. Mere inches apart now, the power, concentration and strength surrounding him felt like a tangible force. Lake wasn't prepared for his intense masculinity. The sensation silenced any further protestations of her innocence in the accident—for the time being.

He rounded the front of the truck, swept the door open, and swung his long frame inside.

"Hold on to her. Brace with your legs."

Matthews maneuvered the truck through a hair-raising U-turn that left Lake squinting. She managed to resist the urge to reach for the "hang on" handle above the door, as they hightailed it back toward Harmony. A few death-defying swerves later, she decided she could do this. She'd just pretend she didn't know who the person next to her was . . . the person who ruined her life. She shook her head. Not helping. Focus, Lake. Focus—on the dog. The heavy dog. Do what you have to do. This dog, this beautiful dog, was counting on them right now.

Lake bit down the explanations that kept rising to her lips. Matthews ignored her, but glanced frequently at his dog and consoled with a, "Hang in there Elle. It'll be okay, girl. It'll be okay."

Once, an, "I came around the corner and—" managed to slip out, but it sounded feeble, even to her ears, as it slammed into the huge block of icy animosity wedged between them.

"Save it." His voice, low and steady, stopped any protestation. It seemed neither of them wanted to upset the patient.

But, as the valley and Harmony came into view, she gave it one more try. Aiming for a calm steadiness she began, "You should know, I—"

"Listen." He cut her off. "Let me concentrate on the road or we'll all go over the edge." His frown deepened. "Don't talk about it now—just let me try to save my dog from your latest calamity."

Your latest calamity.

Uhh. His words were like a punch in the stomach—

Your latest calamity . . .

That about summed it up, all right. Less than a year ago everything in her life was right on track, full steam ahead, next stop—happily ever after, Jeremy by her side. Her photography was getting noticed by the industry. Parents cheering her on . . .

No . . . No, no, no. Her vision blurred. *Don't do it Lake . . . don't go there . . . stop. Full stop.* She would *not* let him see her cry. She made herself so mad at times. The tears—just beneath the surface, ready to flood out. She never allowed herself to let go around River. One of these days, Lake had a feeling the dam would burst—but not here—not in front of Matthews. Maybe out in the forest—alone. Not now.

Force of will, Lake—force of will.

She kept silent after that, concentration focused on keeping a large, injured dog immobile on her lap and holding back a full-blown cry.

As for Matthews, he seemed relieved by her silence. Aside from one sideways look she caught as he made a brief, hands-free call to summon the vet, he didn't look her way again. Lake kept eyes glued to the dog or the sight of Harmony growing closer.

**

Dr. Simon and his assistant met them with a "doggy" gurney as they drove up. It looked pretty much the same as the ones used for humans.

Hawk loosened Lake's stiff arms from the dog, and they hurried into the office and back toward the exam room.

Lake followed, but was cut off by Matthews at the exam room door.

"Go. Just go." Fatigue tinged his voice as he pushed fingers through his hair.

Lake took a step forward extending a hand and tried again. "Let me explain."

"Keep your explanations—and please—from now on—keep away from me," he fired. "Then maybe, just maybe, I'll be able to keep my truck, keep my dog alive and what's left of my peace of mind."

Any remaining conciliatory air sputtered out of Lake's balloon. It was absolutely no use. She had tried, hadn't she? Valiantly. Given him far more effort than he deserved. Let him think whatever he wanted. The man was impossible, worth every ounce of her anger. She answered his fiery scowl with her coolest stare.

Shoulders back, feet apart and hands on hips, she fired her barrage. "All I've been doing *since* we crossed paths is—keeping my explanations. You don't listen. You *won't* listen. Like the night you left my parents in the blizzard. You didn't listen then—you're not listening now. If your dog weren't hurt..."

Lake stopped herself short from spouting off a list of every rotten name she could think of and took a breath. Holding "the hand" in front of his face when he dared to open his mouth, she fired off another barrage, "I hope your dog's all right. Animals don't choose their people. She can't help it if you're a class A, number one, king of the mountain, bull-headed... failure." She finished with, "And I will definitely keep away from you."

With a defiant turn, she marched out the door, leaving Hawk Matthews in her verbal wake.

**

Judgmental... king of the mountain... bullheaded... failure... Hawk realized his mouth was open, poised to speak and he closed it with a grind of his teeth. No one had ever given him "the hand" before.

Even though she was berating him, he couldn't help noticing those eyes of hers—the light glinting through their depths. It reminded him of the frozen waterfalls up in Banff—that otherworld aqua. Haunting.

Stop that thought right there. Those eyes could do damage to a guy—if circumstances were different.

But circumstances weren't.

Guilt swept over him. First, for thinking about Lake's eyes, while Elle was lying hurt in the next room. What was wrong with him? Second—the knowledge that he'd behaved badly. He raked fingers through his hair—but the motion couldn't push the nagging feelings away. She'd wanted to explain what happened. He didn't want to hear it. Deliberately stopped her.

Tough questions confronted Hawk. Questions he knew would come back to haunt him in the middle of the night, when, without daytime distractions, the inescapable specter of truth appears and wraps itself around you so tight you can't ignore it.

They pinched at him now—did he subconsciously want to put Lake McDonald in the role of injurer, because it would be easier for him? Ease his guilt about being unable to save her parents? Would it be easier on him if he could categorize her as a hurtful person, instead of a woman injured by tragedy? A tragedy, despite all his training, he'd been helpless to prevent.

Hawk groaned at the self-revelation. Not one prone to pushing frustrations onto others, it left him with a knot in the pit of his stomach.

He turned on the heel of his black Justin's to rejoin his dog and the Doc, but he couldn't help glancing out the window at Lake's stiff back receding into the distance. Hawk issued a silent prayer—*I could use some help—with a lot of things.*

***

Lake bee-lined it out of Doc Simon's office and across the street. Cutting through an alley, she stomped through every puddle that dared get in her way and headed for her studio. It felt good to let off steam.

Her pace gradually slowed as she realized, in all honesty, she would be distraught too—if she had a dog like Elle and it was hurting. But she wouldn't have been so judgmental. She would have listened. Hopefully, the dog would be all right. Lake would check later, but there was no way she would let Matthews find out.

Matthews. She shook her head and stormed the rest of the way to her studio. No amount of shaking her head and talking to herself would remove their recent encounters from her mind.

What a waste of great cheekbones. In another universe, she would have asked to use him as a model for Wild Wear, a client of hers. A skilled eye couldn't help analyzing that enigmatic look. The camera would love him—great jaw line—dark, full head of hair over dark brows—his mouth—the photographer in her switched off. She couldn't consider his mouth without connecting it with the damaging words that had come out of it.

Jeremy was like that—only blond. Well, and not so muscular. Jeremy had turned out to be like one of those chocolates that look so good, but when you got to the inside—nothing but a gooey mess of yuck. Was there any guy out there with a soft, rich, caramel center?

Stop. How had a professional study of Hawk Matthews's cheekbones turned into a comparison with Jeremy? Or chocolate? Humph . . . Maybe it was all men. Best to turn her thoughts off the course they were traveling. They were both jerks.

Note to self—make sure to raise River to be a different kind of man.

Okay Lake—stop it, reminding herself it was Sunday. Hadn't she been in church a few hours ago? Being this big sister-mom—how was she ever going to do this thing right?

The hurt and pain was still so fresh. Lake considered her silent treatment of God. Sometimes it didn't feel right—like maybe it was wearing her down further. Still—questions hung over her like big, dark clouds. Why, why, why? Her life before last year had been pretty great. She thought she'd appreciated it. Another *calamity* he said . . .

Her mind wandered back to Matthews. She'd be willing to bet, any woman on the receiving end of that voice, in different circumstances, and if the charm were turned on, would pretty much turn to mush. His tone of voice as he comforted his dog—well, it was as smooth as Belgium chocolate. Lake tried to shake it, but it played over and over in her head like one of those songs that won't go away. Annoying. The more she tried to make it stop, the more it stayed.

Think of anything else. Think . . .

Chocolate. Chocolate might do the trick. Always appropriate. At least the thought of chocolate turned her mind elsewhere. Back at the apartment, she searched her kitchen. Nothing. Grrrr. Need chocolate. Need chocolate *now.*

She looked at the clock. Two. River wouldn't be home until five. Plenty of time, she thought as she closed the door and headed to Suzanne's for a piece of her famous Molten Mocha Chocolate Cake. Oh, yeah, that should do it. She'd have chocolate and figure out how to get up to her Jeep. At least the truck issue was solved. Not quite the way she planned, but at least it was done.

A few minutes later, she'd made herself comfortable in a booth at Suzanne's, where she waited for her plate of Molten Mocha stress relief. It was cathartic, watching people stroll by the window, on their way to and from the various interesting shops in the quaint tourist town. Wow, a mini-blizzard yesterday and in the fifties today. This was more like it. People were coming out of hibernation.

She would stop by Sam's office after her chocolate fix and see if he would be available to help solve the problem of the still stranded Jeep.

"A penny?" Suz asked as she set the treat in front of Lake.

Suz was a peach. Before she came home to Harmony, she went through a period of tough times. They had shared experiences during the long winter, over strong cups of tea and anything chocolate. She was originally from Whitefish, a few miles north. She'd gotten out fast after high school, planning to never look back. One little daughter, one loser boyfriend and a whole bunch of life lessons later, she was home again. Her parents had backed her in getting the loan for the diner and she hadn't let them down. She worked hard. Lake admired that.

"You wouldn't believe it if I told you."

Suz looked around, with no one in need of immediate attention, she scooted into the booth opposite Lake and laid the yellow order pad and pencil down on the red Formica. She crossed her forearms on the edge of the table.

"Try me."

Lake focused on the forkful of extreme chocolate cake suspended in the space between them, appreciating its chocolaty lusciousness before launching into the condensed version of yesterday. "In the past twenty-four hours, I took some of the best shots of my career . . . I think. Then I lost the camera . . . ran cross-country from what I thought was a wolf—which turned out to be a dog." She grimaced and continued, "Hawk Matthews's dog." Lake let that much sink in for a few seconds and tapped her pink nails on the red Formica for emphasis. "The fearless leader of Glacier Rapid Retreaters," she finished sarcastically.

Suzanne sighed. "Honey—don't you think—?"

"Don't I think what?"

"Nothing. Never mind, go on with—what you were saying."

She frowned. Suzanne wasn't about to defend Matthews, was she? Suz had a tender heart, but she hadn't been the one who pleaded with Matthews to save her parents. She'd give her a pass on this one. She continued—skimming over the assistance Matthews had provided fishing her out of the stream, segueing quickly to the part about the shortwave radio, ". . . and when I heard his name, and realized who he was—" Lake swallowed to clear the sudden catch in her voice, "I knew I couldn't be stuck there. So, I kind of borrowed his truck—without—uh—actually asking," Lake cringed at Suzanne's expression, but defended her actions, "It was for his own good, Suz. Believe me, neither one of us wanted to be in the same room with the other. I did us both a favor." Lake finished with a right-handed thump, sending the forkful of cake bouncing across the table. A quick move recovered it before it went over the edge.

"Two second rule," and popped it in her mouth as she wiped some molten ooze off the table with her napkin.

Suz put the little yellow pencil she had been playing with behind her ear and raised an eyebrow at Lake, "So, let me get this straight, you figured taking . . . I mean '*borrowing*' Hawk's truck would get you away from him?" Adding, with a shake of her head, "Seems to me, you've forced him to track you down."

Lake's eyes grew bigger. "Definitely *not* my plan. Although, I'm not too worried about his tracking ability—according to my experience." Then added flatly, "He already has his truck back, anyway."

She explained how she found Elle on the side of the road. "Of course, he wouldn't listen to what I had to say. I don't think the word listen is in wonder boy's vocabulary." Lake plopped another forkful of the chocolate mood-fixer into her mouth.

"My goodness lady, you have been busy. Maybe I should have made that serving a double."

"Oh no. This piece is huge. It'll take days to work these calories off, but—oh, so worth it." She closed her eyes in appreciation. "There are times when nothing will do the trick like your Molten cake."

"A girl after my own heart." Suz beamed at the compliment.

The bell tinkled on the café door, interrupting them.

Suz leaned in. Her words were fast and low. "John Colter . . . Hawk Matthews's nemesis. Word is—Hawk thinks he's trying to get his hands on the old Shadow mine." She put a hand on Lake's shoulder as she exited the booth.

"We'll continue this conversation another time." She winked at Lake and turned to the man headed their direction.

Lake turned attention to John Colter—Hawk Matthews's nemesis? That's what Suz had called him. Hmm, not bad looking. Late thirties maybe? Tanned. Had the look of a skier. Lots of good skiing close-by. Broad shoulders. From the looks of his clothes, he didn't spare the bucks on his threads, either. A Denali jacket—every outfitter's top of the line. Lake interned in college for a photographer who did work for Denali Outerwear. Not cheap.

"Hello, John." Suz said cheerfully. "What can I get you this afternoon?"

Now, standing almost beside Lake's table, he smiled, white teeth accentuating the tanned face. "For a start," he smiled at Suzanne, then Lake, "an introduction."

"Oh, sure. Lake, John Colter. John, Lake McDonald." Suzanne raised an eyebrow opposite the side Colter was standing on.

Lake hid any trace of interest from her face as she exchanged greetings with the 'nemesis'.

"Pleased to meet you Mr. Colter." She extended her hand.

Instead of shaking her hand, he held it. "Lake McDonald. Unusual name. Very pleased to meet you. Please, call me John."

"John." Lake nodded and extricated her hand. "Call me Lake."

"I would *like* to call you, Lake."

He smiled at his own cleverness, but it was too practiced for Lake's taste. Part of having a good "eye" was the ability to spot the genuine from the fake. Colter was an easy read—by the way he held her hand and rubbed his thumb over hers. No, it had taken her less than a minute to figure out they were not on the same wavelength.

"May I?" He asked. Not waiting for an answer—he slid into the spot Suzanne had vacated.

Suz took John's order and was off when the doorbell tinkled again.

"I was almost finished. I'm afraid I have to run." She started to scoot from the booth.

"Surely you have time for one cup of coffee? On me?" Colter smiled.

The coffee—on him—might not be a bad idea, but not quite the way he envisioned. He made her uncomfortable. She was about to answer, when, who should walk past the window directly beside them, but Hawk Matthews.

His fiery scowl cut like a laser through the window at them. From his vantage point, it probably appeared as though she and Colter were enjoying a cozy chat and coffee together.

Lake couldn't remember the last time she'd been on the receiving end of such a scowl. Oh—wait a minute. Yes, she could— just this morning from—guess who.

Suddenly, the idea of another cup appealed to her. If it would get Matthews's goat, she'd drink the whole pot with this Colter dude.

"One more cup couldn't hurt." She waved at Suz. "Another tea over here please, Suz?"

"Comin' up."

She would overrule her instincts this time, if it meant a chance to irritate Hawk Matthews further.

Hawk entered the café and surprised Lake by walking straight over to their booth.

"Well, isn't this cozy?"

Colter stared back at him, "What's it to you, Matthews, if I'm enjoying a cup of coffee with my friend?"

"Yeah, well, I wanted to tell your friend here, that my dog is going to be all right. She's banged up, but should be okay. Nothing broken. I spotted you in here and thought

I'd let you know the damage done by the truck was minimal."

She met Matthews stare with her coolest glare, but made no comment. What was the use of trying to explain about his dog again? Instead, she turned a shiny smile toward John Colter.

"This cake is to die for. Whenever I need to get something unpleasant off my mind," she shot a passing glance at Matthews—looming over the table. "Works like magic. Matter of fact, I just enjoyed a piece. It did the trick—until a minute ago." She lifted a menu and feigned interest in it. "Or the pecan rolls . . . hard to decide between the two."

Colter piped in, "Sorry to hear about the dog . . . being okay, that is. That mongrel of yours is a menace."

You could have heard a pine needle drop. By this point, all eyes in the café were turned their direction. Lake noticed Matthews's fist muscles tense. Did he intend to swing at Colter? From the way they were staring at each other, she wondered if she'd have to start ducking. Maybe she was getting in over her head here.

Matthews's hand relaxed, but his jaw muscles clenched even more.

As far as she could tell, the dog was a great animal. Even after only a slight acquaintance, she could see the bond between man and dog—no matter what her personal feelings were toward the human side of the duo.

She hadn't intended to speak to Matthews, but shocked at Colter's cruel comment, words spilled out of her mouth, "Whether you believe it or not, I didn't hit your dog. It appears to be a lovely animal. Dogs can't choose their owners and I'm glad she's going to be okay. But, I don't actually care what *you* think." She added plenty of emphasis to the last part.

Matthews turned his stare from Colter to her, but kept silent.

Poking a stick at a tiger—this is what that must feel like. Much as she would like to annoy him further, it might be best to cut her losses and make an exit. Evidently, this Colter was scum, if his comment toward the dog was any indication. She didn't want to be associated with either one of them, anyway. No white hats here, only black.

"You know, on second thought," she glanced at her watch, "I should run. Glad to have met you, Mr. Colter."

She couldn't force herself to say the standard "nice to have met you", but she was glad she had met him. That was the truth. The whole encounter, however brief, had been illuminating.

"John. Call me John." He smiled a crooked smile. "And don't forget, you said I could call you, Lake."

Very Funny. Ha, ha, thought Lake. What a difference a minor change in inflection could do to the intended meaning of a statement.

"I said you could call me *Lake*," she stressed, adding, "Perhaps we should go back to Ms. McDonald."

She picked up her ticket and slid out of the booth, turning her back on them, leaving John Colter with a smirk and Hawk Matthews with an expression she couldn't quite interpret.

She wasn't going to waste time trying.

FOUR

Bitter Taste

They had *just* met? Hawk jammed his thought process into reverse, attempting to revise the scenario he'd formed about Lake. A scenario he'd evidently not taken the time to properly figure out. Why did he keep jumping to conclusions about her? It wasn't like him.

He adjusted his hat. *Matthews, you're losing it.* She'd insisted she hadn't hit Elle, so who—

"Beautiful girl, isn't she?" John Colter smirked as they watched Lake pay and leave the café, then took a slow, noisy sip of his coffee.

This wasn't the time or the place to settle their differences. Hawk shot Colter a disgusted look and turned to leave.

A figure emerged from the corner booth. Previously out of view, but evidently not out of earshot, Sam Patrick was wearing the same devilish grin he'd sported during some of their most memorable escapades in high school. Hardly fitting for a sheriff, Hawk thought, but he knew Sam's expression spoke more about his long-time friend's ability to see right through him than anything having to do with law enforcement.

Sam must have been listening to the entire exchange. As he walked by, he purposely shoved an elbow into Hawk's back, out of Colter's view. Tipping his Stetson in their direction, he greeted, "Hawk—beautiful spring day—shame to spoil it—arguing." The sheriff continued to the cash register, paid his bill and exited the café, grin still in place.

"What's so funny?" Hawk pressed, a little ticked as he caught up with Sam on the sidewalk.

Sam chuckled. There'd always been good-natured sparring between them. Today evidently, Sam didn't think Hawk was in the proper good-natured spirit. Consequently, Sam seemed to be enjoying it even more.

"What?" Hawk repeated.

"Smooth buddy, real smooth. Yeah—Lake's sure impressed with you. Way to change her opinion, all right. Good for me, though. Thanks."

"What makes you think I care what she thinks of me? Anyway, how do you know Lake McDonald?"

"Not everyone hibernates all winter."

"I've been to town plenty." Hawk repositioned his hat.

"GRRR calls don't count." He frowned at Hawk's scowl. "You know, your face is gonna get stuck like that pretty soon." Then, Sam turned serious. "Listen, I get that you two butted heads the night of the crash, and I know she's not being fair to you—but she's not a bad person. I've gotten to know her a bit. She's trying to cope. Her world's been thrown upside down. She'll figure it out. World-class photographer—like her folks. Moved up here for her little brother, after the accident." Sam shook his head.

They watched her moving away, about a block down the street. Hawk folded his arms across his chest.

"Personally, I don't care if she gets it figured out or not. But professionally, I really wish she'd stop shooting her mouth off—about what a lousy job she thinks I did that night. It was tough enough—" he cleared his throat and stopped talking.

Sam nodded, the grin gone. Hawk didn't need to say any more. Sam knew it had done a number on him—how he'd agonized over halting the search that night—tortured him further when they reached the McDonalds a day and a half later. Both dead.

Both had, what, even under ideal conditions, would most likely have been fatal injuries. But they'd managed a final embrace—and were found frozen that way. The memory could send a shudder through any man involved, even now, months later.

They continued watching Lake in silence for a moment. Hawk spoke first. "Why haven't you mentioned her?"

"Yeah. Sure. Your favorite topic. Hers too. Right." He put a hand on Hawk's shoulder. "Give it time." Then, put his grin back on, attempting to lighten the mood. "Besides—a beautiful woman moves to town—what? I'm supposed to call and let you know? No way, buddy. I've been around you long enough to take whatever head-start I can get."

He shot Sam an incredulous look, "Seriously—have at it," raising his hands in surrender. "No interference from here on this one."

"Right. Listen—don't you have some metal to go pound on? Maybe knock you out of this funk you're in." He pointed a finger at his friend's eyebrows. "Really—frown lines buddy—makes ya look mean. See ya."

"Lake, hold up there." Sam loped off down the sidewalk after her.

What was his friend thinking? That he should make nice with Lake McDonald? Hawk watched them, rubbing at the frown on his forehead.

To be honest with himself, he'd been so concerned about Elle this morning, he could have jumped to the wrong conclusion. Very possible. A growl of frustration rumbled in his throat. If so, at the minimum, she deserved an apology.

When had he become so unreasonable? His grandfather hadn't raised him like this. He'd always considered himself to be fair-minded—magnanimous even. Where was that?

So, now Lake McDonald could add jerk to everything else she thought about him. Yeah, he'd been in rare form where she was concerned. Had he let her explain anything? No. Finding Elle injured on the road—he cringed inwardly as he replayed the scene. She'd tried to explain things. He hadn't let her get a word in edgewise.

And just now—in the diner—assuming she was a friend of Colter's?

That saying about assuming? Yeah, he could be the poster-boy for that one.

He rolled his shoulder and exhaled slowly, trying to release some tension. So far, he'd been wrong about pretty much everything concerning Lake McDonald. He rubbed at the two-day's stubble on his jaw in frustration. She hadn't hit Elle. And she had still helped. Even hating him—she'd still helped.

His mind mounted a futile defense. After chasing that geologist off the ranch yesterday morning, he'd been in rare form. They guy was trying to get core samples from the old mine—again. Between that, the lack of sleep and the abuse his body—and mind—had sustained trying to get to that hiker—or the pieces that were left—last week—

He issued a clumsy prayer—*It's been tough lately. I know it's not much of an excuse. You know I want simple. Seems You have other things in mind. Help me cope. Thanks for Elle. I know she has a lot of people to help yet.*

In his heart, he repeated the pledge he had been making since he was a teenager. *If it's Your will—I will.* The two failed rescues flashed to mind. *I don't understand . . . Give me the strength . . .*

Somber, he watched the scene down the street as Sam opened the door to the sheriff's cruiser for Lake. As they drove away, Hawk knew what he had to do—how to go about it was a different story.

Could he straighten things out? Right now, it seemed next to impossible.

He'd pick up Elle, head back to Shadow, take Sam's suggestion—pound on some metal—and figure it out.

***

It was a welcome turn of events when Sam offered to help her retrieve the Jeep. After a couple miles of amicable small talk about the weather, more pressing questions bubbled to the surface.

"So, what's his deal anyway?" she asked, looking at the road ahead and trying to keep her cool.

Sam didn't look surprised by her question.

"Whose deal, Hawk's or Colter's?"

"Well, both I guess—if you don't mind me asking—seeing as how I have evidently stepped in the middle of something pretty stinky."

Sam gave a sideways smirk.

"Yeah, it's stinky all right . . . and the smell's blowing in from Colter's direction. Thing is," he lifted one hand from the wheel motioning, "you can't arrest a person for having what you think are 'evil intentions'. Oh, don't get me wrong, we're all sure he has designs on the old mine. He's been asking a lot of questions around town, brought in geologists and surveyors, and he's purchased property just outside the conservancy property next to Hawk's. That, and quite a conversation Suzanne overheard in the café, between

Colter and some of his cronies—but, he has yet to do something other than be a major pain in the— Sorry."

Lake smiled, then shook her head wondering, "What about trespassers? Couldn't you arrest them?"

"I could—if that's what Hawk wanted. But, tying them to Colter might be a little tricky. Take you for instance."

Lake winced.

"*You* accidentally wandered onto Hawk's land. They would say the same. It would take a lot of time and money to pursue. Hawk hasn't shown any interest in doing that—yet. He's fed-up with chasing them off, though. You won't get to John Colter that way. Nope, I figure we'll have to wait him out. Either he'll get tired of running into walls or he'll make a bigger move."

"Why is he so sure there's gold there anyway?"

Sam negotiated a particularly tight curve with a stunning view—and a deathly drop—before answering her question.

"Rumor has it, he managed to get a geologist in there who brought out a promising ore sample. That, and well, greed drives people to think and do stupid things. He's greedy. From most reports that old mine has been played out since, well, forever." He frowned and shook his head. "Gold or no gold, it's basically a death trap. It's cost more than one person their life. No one knows that better than Hawk."

That turned her head. "What do you mean?"

Sam glanced Lake's way and continued, "Now that people are nosing around the mine again, Hawk wants to have it permanently sealed. Eliminate the problem once and for all. Implode the shaft under his property. But the permit process to do that takes forever. Especially with explosives and the fact that, while most of the mine lies under Hawk's property, the actual entrance kind of straddles the property line with the Barnes's land. Some weird old survey glitch. She needs be on board too. Mineral rights and a whole slew of other legal stuff. So far, she's been reluctant. You'd think—" His sentence dropped off, but he shook his head, continuing to stare at the road ahead.

"What did you mean; *No one knows that better than Hawk?*"

His frown deepened and he hesitated for a moment, as if considering how to proceed.

"Hawk's father sent him up here, after his wife—Hawk's mother died. He was eight or nine. His mom had cancer. After she died, his dad pretty much fell apart—booze and pills. Things went downhill fast. Sent Hawk up here to live with his wife's father. Yeah, his dad really hit the skids." Sam shook his head. "Sad deal. Anyway, Hawk became friends with a kid, Joey Barnes, who lived on the place next to his grandfather's. Joey's mother, Monica, still lives up there."

Sam inhaled deeply. "I didn't know Hawk very well at the time, but I remember it all from the news and at school. They were out looking for Joey's dog. Couldn't find him anywhere. Then, they came across tracks by the mine. They both knew better than to go in there . . . but two nine-year-old boys worried about a dog . . ." He shook his head.

Lake cringed. She pretty much figured out what was coming next.

"There was a cave-in. Part of the ceiling collapsed. Joey was hit by a timber support. They figured it probably killed him right away. Hawk's leg was caught under the same timber. Took a day to locate them. Almost another day to get them out. Hawk could see Joey the whole time. He never talked about it. I don't think he's gone near the old mine since."

He tilted a glance at her. "Guess it's not too hard to figure why he got involved with GRRR. He's been pretty beat up on the last couple of calls. Still sore I think—more ways than physical. After your folks, well, there was that hiker."

"*Humph*. Maybe he'll figure out he's no good at it—give it up, quit ruining people's lives, find another profession."

Sam's exhale spoke his disappointment. "Lake, I know you've been through a lot, but . . . Hawk's not... well, he's my best friend. I'd trust him with my life." He gave up trying to convince her as the jeep came into view. He shrugged. "There's your Jeep."

***

Lake swallowed her next comment—out of respect for Sam—but, she had to admit—her last statement about Matthews—had left a bitter taste in her mouth. She thanked Sam and hurried to the Jeep.

Driving back, she distracted herself with the question of what to make for supper. River was due home in an hour and she needed to come up with something. Hamburgers and a veg should do tonight. Good thing he wasn't a picky eater. Was he the perfect kid, or what? If she could only be half as good a "mom" as he was a kid . . .

Hard as she tried, she couldn't stop her thoughts from circling back to her earlier conversation with Sam. Of course, he would be sympathetic toward his friend—being old high-school football buddies and all.

But, this new information Sam provided about Hawk Matthews rolled round and round in her head until it ached. A nagging feeling she couldn't quite put her finger on, lingered.

She had to keep in mind that Sam's viewpoint was skewed. The sheriff was a nice guy, but . . . these small towns . . . everybody knows everybody else and everybody else's brother. Stick up for each other. They obviously couldn't see Matthews as clearly as she could—as an unbiased newcomer.

Still mulling as she opened the door to the studio apartment, she headed straight for the little kitchen and pulled out the old, cast-iron skillet, handed down from her grandmother. As she mixed egg, onion, salt and pepper, and her secret ingredient—Worcestershire sauce into the hamburger meat, she mixed the events of the past two days in her mind. It always came down to the truth. Was she the only one able to figure Hawk Matthews out?

Fear. Plain old fear. He was scared that night and it cost her parents their lives. A truth, it seemed, a lot of people in this town didn't want to acknowledge.

***

John Colter took his time finishing his coffee at Suzanne's that afternoon, even ordered another cup while he contemplated the interesting little scene that had played out in front of him.

So, Matthews and the McDonald woman were at odds. Hmm. Another bit of potentially useful information to aid him in his quest to acquire the mine. Matthews had the sheriff in his back pocket. Just his luck they were friends. Everyone around here was so enamored of Matthews. Big hero. But lately, he'd gathered some doubters. Evidently Lake McDonald was one of them.

Years of experience pushing people told him Matthews was close to losing his cool. Maybe he could use this "Lake" to turn the tide in his favor. Ha. This could be good.

He gathered information, that's what he did—and was good at it. But his real specialty was putting it all together in one giant chess game to position his king—King Colter.

His gut told him this new pawn in the game could be a powerful piece if moved correctly. Maybe work her all the way across the board and turn her into his queen. Put Matthews in checkmate. He smiled silently at his analogy and stirred a fourth packet of sugar into his coffee.

Lake McDonald. She was as beautiful as her namesake, and twice as icy. Maybe he'd take a shot at making her boil.

He smiled, then downed another slurp of the syrup he'd concocted.

FIVE

Cooler Meltdown

That's what he was talking about. With a loud thunk, Hawk stacked the last piece of walnut on the pile accumulating at the back of the studio, provoking a sharp bark from Elle, who was recuperating on a blanket across the room, under the worktable. The planks would come in handy for future bases. Walnut made a beautiful base when sanded and oiled. While he often used oak or pine for copper works, he was especially partial to the blend of a stainless-steel piece on a walnut base.

Hawk grabbed the blue chambray shirt he'd tossed on the metal armature of what would someday become a copper elk. Pulling the shirt over sore muscles, he buttoned a couple buttons and walked to the middle of the studio.

Sore muscles aside, it was good to get the place organized again, even if it was frustration that pushed him to it. Maybe he'd catch some decent sleep tonight. The first piece was nearly ready for the Denver show—time to clear space for the next. He'd promised two pieces to Wilderness Wild for the yearly benefit auction. The way things were going, he wished he'd only promised one—seeing as how his muse had deserted him of late—and hadn't turned up under any of the studio debris. But, he was a man of his word and it was for a cause he believed in. He'd make it happen.

Some of his current problems came with the territory. Blessed with a highly visual imagination—and memory—were a great asset when sculpting—not so great trying to erase images of the broken bodies of victims you were unable to help. First, the McDonalds, then, that hiker.

Sure, training had taught him this could happen—and ways to deal. But—the reality of clearing his head of images that appeared, unbidden, in the middle of the night--that was proving to be a different story.

He'd always regrouped in the studio. That's what he needed—get back into the zone. Concentrating on a new design or just making some noise, physically working the metal—always centered him—or had until recently.

Today felt good. He surveyed the studio. Yeah, the answer was here someplace.

Sculpting had grabbed ahold of him as a teenager and never let go. Thoughts flooded back to where it all started— to the art center class his grandfather had enrolled him in— somehow recognizing it might be a good fit for his troubled grand-teen. It saved him. Figured the Lord led him to it through his grandfather—and he would be ever grateful.

Sculpting let him express things he never could have spoken—even with a million words.

And lately, the words he did try were all wrong anyway. Yes, he had frustrations. They swamped him every time he thought about Lake.

He slipped a quilted cover from his latest work—a stylized stainless-steel cougar lying on a polished walnut ledge. The sleek, flowing curves from toe to tail were slowed only by brow, front paws and a few angular muscles. A much-needed feeling of satisfaction washed over him as he considered it, feeling it captured the powerful, yet sleek essence of the animal.

Good to focus on a project that had worked.

Running a hand over the big metal cat, he recalled the Thomas Browne quote "*All things are artificial, for nature is the art of God.*" Nature is the art of God. The Ultimate Artist. Yeah, he celebrated that with his art. In a way, it was his own kind of prayer of praise.

Love of the wilderness permeated his work. This country was at the core of him—part of him—heart and soul. Who he was—is—will be. If he could write poetry about it he would. But he couldn't. His poems were hewn of metal— his verses—steel, bronze and copper—layered with patina and bolted to polished walnut.

Fortunately, others felt the same way. Blessed with many fans and few critics, it enabled him to keep on doing the work he loved—and support causes important to him—like GRRR. Like Wilderness Wild. But critics there were. A few called his work *too abstract*. They just didn't get it. He attempted to capture a spirit ... an essence. All he had to say to his critics— "*Get a camera. Take a picture.*"

Maybe from now on, he'd suggest they hire Lake McDonald.

Speaking of pictures . . . Hawk looked to the worktable where he'd set the camera. Had it survived under the snowdrift where he and Elle found it?

He gently pulled the protective fabric back up over the cougar as curiosity moved him to the camera. He should probably see if it still worked—maybe he'd checkout a few of the photos while he was at it. They might offer insight. See if the McDonald's talents had been passed down to their daughter.

A little mud and a few minor scuffs to the case appeared to be the only damage. He rubbed mud from the logo with his thumb. A newer model by the looks of it—not cheap. Looked like the case had kept the water out. With a camera of this caliber, a waterproof case was a smart investment. He turned it over in his hands, examining, figuring out how it worked. He had a decent camera, but nothing with all these bells and whistles.

Elle wandered over and started sniffing it. He chuckled and held the case out to her for a better sniff. The furry snoop always insisted upon sticking her nose in the middle of anything she sensed concerned him. Hawk let her satisfy herself. After about ten seconds, she gave a satisfied snort.

"Yeah, girl. You remember her. *Little Red Riding Hood was afraid of you.*" He gave an affectionate rub to Elle's head. "You big, bad wolf-dog."

"Grrrwoooof."

A push of a button later, the screen on the back of the camera lit up. Hmm, good case. Let's see . . . menu. He accessed the list and began working his way through the photos.

An hour and a half later, with Elle lost in sleep at his feet, one stunned sculptor emerged from his examination with a new respect for a certain intriguing photographer and her art.

Good job, Hawk. That's where jumping to conclusions will get you, he reprimanded himself. *Right off a cliff. No one's fault but your own.* The dumbfounded expressions Lake McDonald displayed at his accusations the other day had been honest. She must think him a real piece of work.

So . . . try to make things right. But how?

He rubbed a calloused hand across an unshaven jaw. Not much he could do about what she thought of his decisions the night of the plane crash—but he needed to apologize for the way he'd acted the past couple of days.

Hawk rumbled a low sigh at his bull-headedness for not listening to her when Elle was hit. She did deserve an apology.

Question was—would she listen? She hadn't listened to him about her parents—to the impossibility of finding them during that blizzard. Maybe they should call it a draw and just steer clear of each other.

No. His grandfather had raised him differently. He needed to try.

Sam had said to "give it time". His friend's optimism was at a higher set-point than his own. Hawk preferred to think of himself as more realistic.

Whether Sam wanted to admit it or not, his friend still managed to be optimistic about people—even after a stint in Afghanistan. Hawk admired that.

Lake's photos showed she had a talent that deserved respect, as did she, regardless of their history. He might have rescued her from the storm, but had he shown her the respect of listening to her then, or the next day? He'd rushed to judgment. Hypocritical . . . that's what he had been. Refusing to listen to her explanation. Think of how it must be for her, trying to deal with the loss of her parents and now, being responsible for her little brother.

He should cut her some slack. He thought back to the pain of losing his mom, then his dad a short time later. Of course, it was so long ago, he was a kid—but did that kind of thing get any easier? And he had his grandfather to help him through. Lake McDonald had no other close family, from the sounds of it.

He pushed his fingers through his hair. This would take some thought . . . and guidance . . .

She was a photographer—another right-brainer? Hmm. He'd let that angle sit back in his subconscious for a while and simmer.

In an attempt to turn his thoughts away from the subject, he instinctively reached for one of the many ebony pencil stubs lying around. He played with the lines on the paper . . . the lines formed an idea . . . the idea swirled and moved on the page . . . one page turned into another page . . . and another . . . and another.

Sometime during that night, his muse slipped back into the studio.

It was well past one a.m., when, tired but satisfied, Hawk pushed himself away from the drafting board. The big, modified barn doors creaked and groaned as if complaining to be put to work at the late hour.

He walked a few steps out into crisp, Montana night. Elle led the way through the large, empty yard, stopping a little way out to stretch, accompanied by a doggy grunt, still moving slowly from her highway encounter.

"You said it, girl." He patted at the dog. "Why do you let me stay out so late?" Stretching arms and back fully, Hawk breathed deeply of the heady elixir of fir trees and wilderness. The sky glistened this moonless night, not a cloud in sight. Starlight energized him. The diamond necklace of the Milky Way—laid on this midnight blue Montana sky. Could any jewels a woman wore ever compare?

Never.

Good to be well away from the eternal daytime that city lights forced on a guy. He'd never pollute this beauty with a security light. He reached down and patted Elle's uninjured shoulder. She was all the security system he needed.

He buttoned his shirt the rest of the way and sat down on the porch steps of the cabin for a time, one arm draped over Elle, the other across his knee, enjoying the Montana night and its sounds. A cool breeze shushed its way over the blanket of fir trees. Crickets chirped their rhythmic mantra. A call sounded . . . he and Elle both turned to listen . . . to the west of the river, a Great Horned Owl hooted its eternal question.

Closer now, more sounds scuffled in the dark, off to the side of the yard. Elle's ears perked up first, then laid flat, as she uttered a soft but serious growl.

Hawk chuckled. Probably her nemesis, an old, cagey raccoon he'd nicknamed—*Toes*—for the footprints the sneaky animal left all over his stuff. Toes was relentless in his attempts at raiding—the cabin, the truck, the studio.

"It's okay girl, calm down. Why don't you give old Toes one of your barks—scare him off?"

Recognizing the word "bark", the dog immediately obliged with an enthusiastic, "Rrruuufff", followed by a half-dozen more.

Hawk patted her back. "Enough, enough. That should take care of him for tonight."

The barking tapered off into a soft growl, punctuated at the end with a snort.

He sat on the steps for a few more minutes, full of thankfulness about being right where he was—appreciating the tranquility of the moment.

But, there it was again. That feeling that kept gnawing at him. All too common lately. Maybe just a low point after the McDonald fiasco. He pulled in another deep drink of the mountain air and exhaled slowly.

Life—so fragile—can end so quickly.

Was it too much to ask, for someone to share what time you had? Besides Elle, of course. He rubbed the dog between the ears. Well, maybe it wasn't meant to be for him. Women had certainly let him down in the past—or he'd let them down. Suppose it all depends on perspective.

Was there a woman out there who could understand him and this place, without trying to convince him to move to *civilization*? Hawk pushed the thought away and soaked in the Montana night for a few more minutes, then, he and Elle entered the cabin.

For a long time, he laid on the king-sized bed and stared out the window, gaze still cast on the stars glimmering above the treetops, waiting for the blanket of sleep to cover his troubled thoughts. When it finally came, it was interrupted by the dream of arguing with Lake McDonald. Not that the dream was anything new—he'd dreamed of the crash and that night many times. But now they were worse. Now, instead of trying to reason with a voice on the phone—there were haunting blue eyes and an unforgettable face connected to the pleading voice.

***

Lake tossed and turned, then turned and tossed—a strange electricity filling the night. Eventually, she gave up trying to sleep. Slipping from the covers, she padded barefoot to the kitchen.

Maybe a cup of chai . . .

In the soft light from the stove hood, she proceeded methodically, adding spices to the boiling water. Soon, soothing aromas of cinnamon, cloves, cardamom pods, pepper, and sliced ginger wafted around her. After simmering the brew for ten minutes, Lake added sugar and milk and covered the mixture, brought it back to simmer, then removed it from the heat and added her favorite Darjeeling tea leaves. A late-night ritual she could perform by heart—and had, many times over during the past few months—when specters of last fall's tragedy rose, unbidden from the ashes of her memory.

She poured the comforting mixture into the little violet-covered teacup. It had been a present from her grandmother on her sixth birthday—filled with candy at the time. She stirred and sipped the sweet, spicy liquid and gradually relaxed.

It would be good to get back to work tomorrow. Throw herself into a project. Cathartic to get—into the zone.

The only problem with this thought being, it sneaked its way back around to the lost camera and the *Snowshine on Shadow* content it held.

Arrrgh. The camera, while expensive, could be replaced—the magical moment in time she had captured could not. Lake sighed. There went relaxed. She did form a new plan though. Perhaps she could enlist Sam's help. Surely Matthews would allow the sheriff a look around the property.

This train of thought was not bound for "Dreamland Station" either, Lake mused and finished the chai. She headed back to bed, vowing to focus her thoughts on faraway places, finally drifting off while remembering a photo session for *Australia Today* magazine, on the beach near Sydney harbor . . . which somehow became oddly mixed with glittering air and a tall man with compelling eyes a smoldering shade of amber.

***

After getting River off to school the next morning, Lake thought about his approaching summer vacation. She considered the timing as she tried to set a schedule for herself. Her alone days would be limited during June, July and August. River was great company and Lake thoroughly enjoyed having him with her in the studio, but, work did not progress as quickly. Some shoots he could accompany her on, others not.

River expressed a real interest in the work she was doing, and Lake intended to let him tag along whenever possible. So many questions in that little head of his. Yes, Lake thought as a satisfied smile crept over her face, there was a strong possibility little bro would follow right along in the family tradition. He already begged until Lake bought him a simple camera.

River worked at putting his own book together, while Lake worked on hers. She was thinking of having his pictures professionally bound for him, as a surprise.

She forced her attention back to the large, four by eight pine worktable full of proofs spread out before her, trying to work out the flow.

Lake gave it a good hour before giving up. The flow wasn't flowing. Almost nine a.m., and the only major thing she'd decided was that she needed a cup of coffee. Shoving the photos aside, she rubbed bleary eyes. Time for a break. Coffee. Strong coffee . . . And umm . . . maybe Suzanne would have one of those pecan rolls left. She could almost taste it right now, freshly baked, oozing sticky caramel and pecans.

Yeah—caffeine and sugar—maybe after an infusion, she could brainstorm a way to recover the missing camera. She grabbed her denim jacket from a peg by the door, hurried down the street and was soon ogling the array of goodies at Suz's counter.

"Mornin' Lake." She smiled and pulled a plate from the shelf behind her. "Saved a pecan roll for you. Usual coffee?"

Lake nodded. "I'm getting too predictable."

Suzanne winked and added, "Gonna stay, or should I bag it?"

"You know, I think I'll grab a booth. All I've been doing is spinning my wheels this morning. A few minutes away from the studio would do me good."

Lake looked around for an empty booth, but her spirits plummeted when she spotted a group halfway down the aisle to her left. It was Hawk Matthews, having breakfast with Sam and a few other men. Her mood turned dark.

"On second thought, make that to go. I see the fearless leader of Glacier Rapid *Retreaters* is here. Wouldn't want to interrupt an *escape* planning session." She got the shot off and hoped it was loud enough for Matthews to hear.

From the glare he sent her direction ... Bullseye.

***

That's it. Hawk's adrenaline surged. Any intentions of apologizing to Lake McDonald disintegrated. How long was he supposed to endure this venom from her? And here, in front of the team. Seven pairs of eyes turned his direction. Sure—she lost her parents. She was having a hard time with it. He got that. He'd been there himself. But continuing to bad-mouth him, all over town ... *C'mon ... really ... how much more?*

But—she had helped Elle when the dog was hurt. She was maddening ... frustrating ...

He narrowed his gaze and watched her out of the corner of his eye. The aroma of the eggs, sausage and freshly brewed coffee in front of him, so mouth-watering five minutes ago, now turned his stomach. She was at it again ... something derogatory to Suzanne. He heard his name and another jibe.

The hate in her eyes could kill without a weapon.

It was torture. Slow torture. Every comment that crept its way back to him twisted the knife of failure deeper into his gut. Goading him.

Hadn't he told himself, just the other night, to exercise compassion . . . empathy . . . to endure . . . remember that she was suffering?

But so was he.

He snapped. Right. Okay. If she wanted this, so be it. They'd have it out—but not in front of Suzanne's cash register.

"Someone needs to dam up the poison pouring out of Lake McDonald," he uttered through gritted teeth. His blue-jeaned thigh hit the table as he stood, setting the silverware jumping and Sam's coffee crookedly spinning over, flooding onto the sheriff's crisp, tan shirt.

"Hawk. No." Sam stood too, momentarily distracted by the hot coffee.

With an adroit move that hearkened back to their football days, he evaded Sam's hand as it shot out to stop him and stood before Lake in seconds. Hands firmly on her shoulders, he ushered a stunned Lake through the swinging silver doors behind the counter into the back room, past trays of pink cupcakes with colorful sprinkles, past stacks of cream colored plates—make that pieces of cream colored plates. He'd pay Suzanne later for the stack that got in the way of his elbow. He opened the metal door to the cooler and pressed Lake into the cold room, still holding her shoulder, deftly avoiding a kick sent in the direction of his shin.

Sam wasn't far behind. "Hawk. Watch yourself. Let her go," came his warning. The sheriff's arm stopped the cooler door from closing.

"Yeah." He answered Sam without taking his eyes from Lake's and dropped his hands to his sides. "You know I'm not going to hurt her."

"Yes—but she doesn't."

His friend's words hit the mark.

"I should have you arrested," Lake hissed the words. "Sheriff, this man assaulted me."

"You okay, Lake? Listen—let's dial things down a few notches here," Sam started.

Hawk interrupted. "We need to talk." He ground the words at her.

She narrowed her stare at him. "All right," came her answer, cold as her expression. Then to Sam, "I'm not hurt Sheriff. It's all right—but please, stay by the door," she finished, not lowering her defiant stare one notch.

The shelves in Suzanne's little eight by twelve, stainless-steel cooler vibrated with the electricity. Sam hesitated while he appraised them both. Satisfied, he nodded. "I'll be right outside the door." He looked from one to the other, assessing, then commanding, "Talk."

The door clicked softly shut.

"We need to straighten things out. Right here—right now."

His stare bounced off the hate in her eyes like sunlight off ice.

"I really have nothing to say to the man responsible for my parents' deaths."

He scowled at her. "You seem to have plenty to say—when my back is turned. Let's get it said to my face—here and now. If you have the guts."

"Don't touch me." Lake warned as Hawk leaned closer.

"I won't touch you." The revulsion in his voice was not lost on her. He waited for Lake to say something, anything, but she didn't make a sound, just sustained her glare.

He'd be happy to start. "Okay. If you won't talk, then you're gonna listen—and listen good. I've had it with the poison coming out of that mouth of yours—about how I handled the rescue."

She rolled her eyes and huffed a, "Rescue?! *What* rescue?"

He pushed his hands through his hair in frustration, then, slapped them to the cool metal of the walls on each side of her shoulders. Lake flinched.

"I – did – everything – in – my – power – to find your parents that night. Quinn broke his femur, we almost lost him. It was time to call everyone in. I- had- no- choice."

"You were scared." She spat at him.

Hawk muttered some French. "You bet I was . . . and so was every man out there. You'd be a fool not to be." He inhaled deeply of the cooler air, gathering his thoughts until he calmed. "For heaven's sake Lake," He shook his head in emphasis, but didn't lower his gaze, "we'd had ten inches of snow—we got twelve more after that. The winds were pushing sixty. I don't control the weather."

"You gave up. Why should you care . . . they weren't your parents?"

He sighed and gave her a hard look. "It was the first search I've ever had to call for weather. Do you think a decision like that doesn't haunt you?" Both his face and his voice softened, "I knew your parents Lake. Worked with them once. Liked them. Do you know how hard—?"

His voice trailed off as a realization avalanche rolled over him. The realization he knew Lake McDonald hadn't faced yet.

It changed everything.

He searched Lake's face with his newfound insight, "But that's not the real problem, is it? You're not brave enough to face the real issue."

Lake narrowed her eyes. "What are you talking about—I know just what happened out there. You got scared—"

There was a moment of silence as Hawk searched the blue eyes.

"Who's scared, Lake?"

She stared at him.

Hawk pressed on. "Like I said. I don't control the weather." He leaned forward. "But that's who you're really mad at, isn't it—the One who can control the weather—I'm just a convenient place to vent because you haven't had the guts to confront who you're really mad at—who you really blame."

"You . . . you don't know what you're talking about."

"Don't I?" He searched her face.

At that moment, all the frustration he had toward Lake McDonald—all the pain she had caused him—drained away. It turned to . . . pity? Sympathy? No. A blend he couldn't quite put his finger on. She was so full of hate and hurt. Hawk dove deeper into blue eyes, trying to capture, put a name to what he felt. She was a mess—one beautiful mess—a mess that was clouding his days and haunting his nights.

"I lost my parents . . ." he said quietly. "I was mad at God." His hands dropped from the cool wall beside her shoulders and he stood his full six-foot three frame solidly in front of her. "Straighten it out with Him—and leave me out of it." He finished firmly.

That struck a nerve. He could see it happening. Her icy stare cracked.

He watched, mesmerized, as one glistening drop slipped down a flushed cheek and ran around the curve and tremble of a soft lip. That's when the second revelation avalanche rolled over Hawk Matthews. Gave him a—weak in the knees feeling he hadn't felt in a—well, he couldn't say he'd ever felt this—

Dear God in heaven—he wanted to kiss her. Wanted to kiss her in the worst way. Wanted to kiss her more than he had ever wanted to kiss a woman in his life. Wanted to wrap his arms around her and hold her till she didn't hurt anymore. Till he didn't hurt anymore.

It shocked him to his core. He froze.

Hawk forced his gaze from her lips back to her eyes. Pooling tears spilled down her cheeks. Then, as her gaze dropped to his mouth . . . she drifted closer . . . looking so desperate. His own eyes start to sting.

Neither breathed.

Not a man to break promises, Hawk broke one then—big time—moving his hands gently to the sides of her face, his thumbs tenderly wiping the tears from her flushed cheeks.

The next thing he knew, the salt of her tears was on his lips—tasting her pain as he kissed a tear away. With a groan of surrender, he moved an arm around her back as the other hand pushed through her hair to cradle her head. A frown creased his brow as he pulled her to him and pressed his lips to hers. Lake's own soft sound registered in his hearing as she moved into the kiss. Her arms circled him in response—a desperate pain seeming to release its hold—his—hers—theirs—who could tell for sure—neither thinking—only feeling.

Hawk could feel her heart pounding through her chest—or was that his?

The cooler door squeaked open slightly. "You two workin' things ou . . . Uh, I guess sooooo." Sam's voice trailed off on an incredulous note as he let the door click shut again.

The spell broken, color drained from Lake's face, leaving her with the look of a deer in headlights, tear trails smudged down her cheeks. With a faint sound of shock, she pushed away from Hawk and shot out the cooler door, shoving past Sam.

The confounded sheriff turned after her. "Lake?"

She waved an arm behind her in the universal—go away—motion, shaking her head as she ran through broken plates and spilled cupcakes, out the swinging stainless doors. They heard Suzanne's "Lake . . . honey . . ." then the bell on the front door as she fled the café.

***

To say that work stagnated for the next few days was quite an understatement. Every morning, best intentions in hand, she got River off to school and attempted to throw herself into *Timeframes*—and each day disintegrated into a repeat of the day before—elbows on work table, chin resting in palms, a cup of cold, spiced chai and contemplation of a life that was getting her nowhere. Oh, she kept up the charade for River's sake, but that's all it was—a charade.

The scene with Hawk in Suz's cooler played on an endless, unforgiving loop through her mind. What she would give for a switch that would turn it off. Night or day, it didn't matter. Could you in fact, die of embarrassment? She had to be getting close.

Hiding out. That's what she was doing. It wasn't like her. Lake's head settled in her palm as she sipped a bit of the cold chai. Why? How had she ended up in Hawk Matthews's arms? Well, more than his arms. That kiss. Goosebumps shivered their way up her arms. She could feel her ears pinking at the thought. But, oh—there had been such a connection in that moment. Lake rubbed her forehead. What an absolute traitor she was. Get a little emotional and fall all over your worst enemy.

That's when, that pesky voice inside her head, or heart, whichever it was—that annoying one you try to ignore when you know you shouldn't—that one—started up again. Louder and louder. Matter of fact, since the scene in Suz's cooler, it wouldn't shut up.

She groaned and laid her forehead down on the blessed coolness of the worktable and reached over to turn off the radio. Trying to mask the voice with noise hadn't worked. Another groan. Her parents had brought her up to be truthful. Truth was the hallmark of a good photographer . . . a good person, for that matter. This game of chess she was playing with truth—denial would never win. She should know better—but it was so hard. Consciously or subconsciously, making Hawk Matthews the bad guy had been her easy-way out—or so she thought.

It didn't feel so easy anymore.

He'd been right on the money. Had named the real reason for her embarrassment. Seeking relief from her own fog of pain, she had inflicted pain on another. She had been unfair, she winced inwardly—horribly unfair, to him.

Oh, God . . .why? The cry, buried deep in her heart surfaced again, but this time, it took breath.

Lake pushed herself away from the table and slowly stood. Realizing what she had to do, she headed upstairs to her little bedroom. There, she hesitated in front of the antique mahogany dresser. The reflection in its faded silver mirror, showed a woman with truth on her face. She stared back at the stark accusation.

She moved her focus to the bottom drawer—to face a different kind of reflection. That's where she'd buried it—the same day she'd buried her parents. Stuffed it under a couple of old shirts she never wore anymore—effectively shut away.

Or so she thought. But truth cannot be imprisoned. She couldn't purge the knowledge from her heart. Couldn't bury it in the bottom drawer and certainly couldn't lock it away forever.

Face-it Lake.

I still don't understand . . . just feel so broken . . . help me . . . deal with . . . all of this. Give me strength.

Taking hold of the tarnished brass handles, she pulled the drawer open, pushed the old shirts aside, picked up her long-neglected Bible and started down a new path.

***

Hawk's last few steps to Lake's studio progressed at a slower and slower pace. He hesitated in front of the door and turned to look over the rooftops of Harmony's shops, over the firs behind them, out toward the mountains, considering. Over the past ten years or so, he'd been involved in more than his fair share of dicey situations. He'd repelled down some gut-wrenching cliffs and clawed his way up again, injured party in tow. He'd jumped out of airplanes, faced surly bears and even delivered a wilderness baby—and never felt any of it in his knees. So, what *was* it about this woman that made them feel like rubber?

Maybe the fact he'd lost it in the cooler? His teeth clenched. What had come over him?

Shake it off man. Hawk composed himself and walked the last few steps to the door. He had intended to return her camera after the last GRRR meeting, but, considering how events unfolded that day in the diner—definitely best to postpone.

So, here he was, three days later, camera in hand, along with a coffee and a paper sack containing a pecan roll that Suz had assured him was Lake's favorite—ready to make amends for his impulsive behavior. Not so much for the feelings he felt, but for the moment—and way—he'd chosen to express them. Lake had been so vulnerable that day, he should have been stronger . . . should have taken time to . . .

Yeah. Shoulda', coulda', woulda' . . . didn't.

No going back now. With his free hand, he grabbed the doorknob and entered the studio, slowly, not knowing for certain if he'd meet with a heavy object lobbed in his direction.

He needn't have worried. No sign of her.

He took a good look around. Strange. The studio was unlocked, photographs spread all over the table, computer still on. Wherever she went, it looked like she'd be back in a few minutes.

Hawk set the sack with her camera on the worktable and the coffee and pecan roll far away from her photos, on a side table. It wouldn't be much of a peace offering if he spilled coffee on her project. He walked over to the front window and waited, hands on hips, watching people pass on the street. Maybe she wasn't coming back soon.

She should lock her door.

After five minutes of shifting from one foot to the other, he noticed Sam going into his office across the street and decided to leave.

Maybe it would be better to have the picture message he left on the camera speak for him, anyway. Hawk congratulated himself again on the brainstorm of adding the photo to the camera. Right. Let that pave the way. She had a soft spot for Elle. Maybe that would work in his favor. The more he thought about it, the better he liked the idea anyway. All he was going to do today was drop the camera off and mention that he added something at the end.

Hawk readjusted his bark colored Stetson and headed for the sheriff's office.

***

Lake spent over two hours that morning reacquainting herself with favorite passages, ending with her father's and her favorite, the twenty-third Psalm.

She was no closer to the answers she craved and probably never would be while in this world, but, in her heart, she felt she'd taken the first few steps.

A little before eleven a.m., Lake moved back downstairs, and was met by the amazing smell of her favorite Colombian coffee and . . . she sniffed sharply . . . a fresh baked roll?? With a frown, her eyes scanned the room for the heavenly aroma's source. Through the front window, she caught sight of the broad-shouldered back of Hawk Matthews crossing the street, headed toward Sam's office.

Note to self—get that bell for the front door.

What was up? Hawk—here in the studio? She zeroed in on the origin of the tantalizing aromas on the desk by her computer.

Huh . . . Curious. She looked out the window again as he disappeared into Sam's office. Lake blinked a few times considering what this meant.

A peace offering?

Hmm. No sense wasting a perfectly good cup of coffee and pecan roll. Lake sniffed the sack. No more skipping breakfasts, she was ravenous as a wild dog. It was too much to resist. With another quick glance to the window, she tore into the sack.

The sweet, gooeyness melted in her mouth and the strong, black coffee made for an excellent chaser. It would be easier to determine what this was about if she had some fuel in her, right? So, Hawk had been here . . .

That was when she spied another sack sitting on the worktable next to the *Timeframe* photos.

What? Lake worked the sack open with her unsticky hand. The sight of the contents sent her into a coughing fit when a bite of roll stuck in her throat. The rest of the roll tumbled to the floor. She moved away from the worktable. The coffee almost followed the roll, but she managed to get it settled on a stool, away from the proofs.

Not believing her eyes she rushed to the sink and washed pecan roll goo from her hands, making little excited noises as she sped along, then hurried back to the sack.

Christmas in April—her camera. She hugged it like a long-lost friend. *How* had he . . . *where* had he . . . *why* had he?

Lake raised her eyes. *Thank you.* Then, turned them out the window again, reformulating the picture of the camera's rescuer walking across the street . . . *And thank you, Hawk Matthews.*

Forcing her attention back to the matter at hand, she addressed the next question. Could her photos still be intact? Lake had high hopes, since she had specifically ordered a *waterproof* case, not merely a *water-resistant* one.

The camera turned on immediately. A good sign. She walked over to her computer desk and sat down, eyes stilled glued to the camera's screen.

"Yes. Yyyyyyes. YES."

Lake wasn't much of a dancer, but that day she choreographed one lively, spontaneous, happy dance. As she reviewed the camera's files, she discovered that all appeared to be intact.

She slipped the stick from the camera into the computer.

"You're not getting away from me again," she told the "Sunshine on Shadow" photographs and quickly made not one but *two* backups. The next four hours were spent examining and making adjustments to some of them. Were they as great as she remembered?

Even better. She couldn't remember being more excited about a set of photos. Her eyes squeezed shut. *Mom and Dad, do you see this?*

Goosebumps—big time. A feeling came over her that she couldn't explain—like they *did* know. She felt it. *Well Lake, wasn't that what you professed to believe all your life?* But, truth be told, what had happened to all that belief when faced with her worst crisis?

Mulling this over, Lake almost overlooked the extra photo that had been added to the very end of the file of pictures. Squinting, she looked closer at the tiny icon, showing what looked like a picture of Hawk beside Elle and a . . . sign? Puzzled she clicked to enlarge it.

There sat Hawk Matthews, on the front steps of his cabin, devastating smile on his face, one arm draped over Elle, who was grinning her best doggy grin, Hawk's other hand holding a sign that read, "Wilderness Survival Class - Community College - Sign Up", and a phone number.

SIX

Photo Frame

Hawk left the photography studio and headed toward Sam's office that morning feeling pretty satisfied with his plan. Upbeat. Hopeful. Good to feel those feelings again—until John Colter ran smack into him on his way out of the sheriff's office.

What was Colter doing in the Sam's office?

"Watch where you're going Matthews," Colter growled.

"You don't own the sidewalk." Hawk ground back.

Colter backed up a little and smiled his crooked smile, "Give me a little time."

"You've taken up too much of my time lately." Hawk narrowed his stare. "But, tell you what, I'm feeling generous today, I'll give you two seconds to get out of my way."

"Gladly." Colter moved aside with an exaggerated gesture. "I don't want to delay your talk with the sheriff. I do believe that he's anxious to talk to you, about that *sheep killing mongrel* of yours." With a self-satisfied chuckle, Colter sauntered down the sidewalk, still chuckling.

"What the—?" He didn't finish the statement as he met Sam at the door.

"What's Colter talking about?" Hawk asked, concern creasing his brow. Sam looked grim.

"You'd better come inside. We'll talk there."

They both gave a brief glance at Colter's receding figure and headed into the Sheriff's office.

Sam moved to his desk and sat, motioning Hawk to one of the chairs in front of the desk. Sam looked mighty uncomfortable. What was Colter stirring up now? Hawk had a pang of sympathy for his longtime friend. As sheriff, Sam had to follow procedure. At least he could tell Colter exactly what he thought of him. Sam didn't have that luxury. He knew Sam better than anyone. Two guys couldn't have a friendship pushing twenty years and not read the other guys opinions well. He marveled at Sam's patience.

"What's he talking about—*sheep killing mongrel?*"

"Come in. Sit." Sam was looking more uncomfortable by the second, kicking up Hawk's adrenaline another couple of notches.

"Yeah, a, well . . . I need to ask you a few things Hawk . . . about Elle, that might tic you off, but I need to get some info. It's all part of the job." Sam motioned for Hawk to sit again.

"John Colter has filed a complaint against you. Well, technically—you as the owner of Elle. You know that land he bought west of Shadow?" Hawk nodded and Sam continued, "Well, he went and put sheep on it." Sam tossed his Stetson onto a pile of papers on the desk, put his hands on his hips and continued, "He's claiming Elle has been over there—that she killed a number of lambs."

Hawk let out a hoot of a laugh, but stopped short when Sam didn't join in.

"You are joking . . . Elle? My dog. My dog, Elle?" At Sam's silence he got serious. Fast. "That's ridiculous and you know it."

"I do know it, but the thing is, he showed up with these." Sam shook his head and shrugged, hesitating a little before he pushed the photos across the desk at him.

Hawk looked down at the stack of photos, then raised an eyebrow at his friend.

"You need to look at those." Sam dipped his head at the photos.

"Why are you letting that creep manipulate you like this?" Hawk's mood darkened as he scowled his way through the stack of photos, then tossed them back on the desk and leaned back in the chair. Seven photographs, showing what looked like Elle chasing the flock. Even more condemning for the dog, were two grisly ones, that looked like her, standing over what used to be lambs, but had been reduced to small piles of bloody wool and bone.

"This is nuts." He shoved the photos back at Sam. "It's not her. A lot of dogs look similar. It's not her. She would never . . ."

"Yeah, I know. But it definitely does look like her." Sam thumbed through the stack again. "You have to admit . . ." He pointed down to a couple of the most damaging photos. "Look at the dark band around this left hind leg and toward the tip of her tail. The dark ear tips." Sam looked at him and shook his head. Elle was family. Sam should understand. His dog, a lovable but usually inert bloodhound named Slug, was family to him, too.

Sam continued, "This doesn't look good."

His temper flared. "I don't care what it looks like. It's garbage and you should know it."

"I have to deal with facts, Hawk."

"The fact is, you should know it." Hawk fired back.

"Does Elle have free run of the area?"

"You've got to be joking. Hawk crossed his arms and leaned back in the chair. "Out where I am? C'mon. You know the answer to that. Of course, she does. How many times have you brought Slug out to my place and they've chased each other around? Elle chases Toes off the place all the time . . . the occasional rabbit . . . barks at deer that wander in. She always stays close. Never goes much farther than the main road unless I'm with her. I wouldn't let her out if she did. She's never been gone on her own long enough to make it clear over to Colter's property. That would take her . . . an hour minimum, round-trip. And look at the blood . . . she'd have it all over her . . ." Hawk rubbed the back of his neck and snorted. "Never happened. No way. No how."

"Well . . . I know you're not gonna like this, but I may have to come out and pick up Elle for a while. Till this gets sorted out."

The chair made a jarring scrape as Hawk stood and glared at Sam. "You could try."

Sam stood his ground, but sighed deeply. "Listen, Hawk. Do you think I enjoy this? This is the last thing in the world I want to do. But I'm not fooling around here. This is serious. You're going to have to find a way to prove where she was at these times." He pushed a list at Hawk. "*I* can't explain these away on my own." He threw a frustrated glance to the photos on the desk.

Hawk grabbed the list from Sam's hand. "He's dumping garbage on me. What can he hope to gain from this?"

Sam reflected. "Well, I don't know anything for sure, but maybe he's going to start harassing you with lawsuits . . . Did you ever think of that?"

"Maybe . . . Or how about turning friends against each other? Ever think of that?

Sam tilted his head, considering. "You might have something there." He rubbed his brow.

"This is nuts." Hawk gave another disgusted look at the list, and Sam, then left the office with an, "I'll get back to you."

Hawk left the sheriff's office wondering what he had ever done in his life to deserve the plague of John Colter.

***

Lake tried to steady her emotions. Brimming with gratitude at the return of the lost camera—but more than that—she was left in wonder by Hawk. After how she deliberately misjudged him . . . made him the target of her scorn . . . He said he lost his parents . . . that he understood. Could he really? Was his spirit generous enough to forgive her?

Lake sighed and studied the camera. She needed to express her gratitude to someone in person. River was in school. Hawk was probably out of town by now. Lake grabbed her jacket and headed down toward the café to tell Suzanne the good news. Come to think of it, Fran usually had lunch there, too.

As she walked down the sidewalk, she spotted Hawk's truck. He was still in town—and there he was, leaving the sheriff's office. Even better. She gathered up her courage and called out to him.

"Hawk." No response. Crossing the street, she called a little louder, "Hawk." He seemed in a hurry, thoughts wrapped up in the piece of paper he held.

The second shout caught his attention and he looked up, mind apparently still on the paper.

Lake, a little out of breath from hurrying, started enthusiastically, "Oh, I'm so glad I caught you. You can't imagine . . . I mean . . . how grateful I am—for finding my camera. You don't know how important it is to me—and River."

He was watching and listening, but, after the whole cooler episode, it wasn't quite the response Lake expected. No smile. Nothing. Maybe she had read too much into the whole thing. A heat of the moment mistake. Feeling foolish, she started to back-peddle as fast a she could.

"Look—uh . . . You were right. I *know* we got off on the wrong foot . . . You can't know how . . . how awful I feel . . . about—" Lake's hands went out in front of her, palms up. She was seriously stumbling now. Why didn't he help her out here? "but I really owe you a *thanks* for finding my camera and . . ."

"Uh, yeah, sure—glad to do it." He stared down at the paper in his hand, then, continued with a stiff smile, "A . . . listen, I'm in kind of a hurry right now." His troubled gaze met her confused one, then dropped back to the paper he held. "I'm sorry. We'll talk again—soon. Sorry."

Without looking up, he tipped his Stetson in the characteristic western gesture, nodded and strode toward his truck, still consumed by the piece of paper he held.

"Uh, okay . . . sure," she ended up speaking at the broad shoulders. Lake stood there for a moment wondering what had just happened, then nodded and proceeded into the sheriff's office. What in the world? She hadn't expected this kind of reaction. This wasn't the same smiling cowboy sitting with his dog and a sign on the cabin steps . . . or the passionate truth teller pouring his heart out in Suz's cooler.

Lake walked absently into Sam's office, giving another puzzled look toward the silver truck as she grabbed the old brass knob and opened the door. Sam sat behind the mammoth, well-worn mahogany desk, which must have been there since the dawn of sheriffs. His brows knitted in concentration as he stared at a pile of photographs. He looked up with an expression similar to the one she'd encountered on Hawk's face.

"Hey, Sam. Got a minute?"

The sheriff's face relaxed a bit. "For you Lake, always. What's up?"

What was going on? Considering Sam's expression, and after another quick look toward the street, she turned the question on him.

"You tell me. I just ran into Hawk Matthews, coming out of here. He found my camera, by the way." She flashed a smile. "But when I tried to thank him, well, I think he was in another world."

They watched Hawk's silver truck as it passed by the front windows, heading out of town.

"Yeah, you could say that."

As a photographer, her eyes didn't miss much. Oh—well—other than mixing up snow covered dogs and wolves, she thought wryly. Her eyes went to the photos on Sam's desk.

She motioned to them. That looks like . . . Hawk's dog." She squinted from her upside-down view. "Is it?"

"Well, now—that's the problem. Sure looks like her, doesn't it?"

"And . . . what are those?" she cocked her head and squinted harder.

"What's left of sheep." He rubbed his eyes wearily.

"Eeeeeuw." Her face scrunched. "Where did these come from? When did this happen?" She shook her head. "You don't really think Hawk's dog . . . or, do you?" Confusing. "The dog didn't seem to have a mean bone in its body. She's . . . a rescue dog for heaven's sake. I thought her pretty mellow."

"I'm having a hard time believing it, too. An *impossible* time . . . Yet . . ." His hand swept above the photos and he shook his head in bewilderment. "I don't understand it. I've known that dog for years and *never* any indication of tendencies like this" Sam rubbed his eyes again. "I don't get it."

Lake continued to look down at the photos. Something was bothering her.

She took the chair in front of Sam's desk.

"Mind if I take a look?"

"Well, seeing as how you've already seen them. It is an ongoing investigation, though. I'll ask you to keep it confidential, but, I could use a consultant."

"I think you should let me look." She told him seriously, eyes still glued to the top photo.

"Go ahead. You're the expert." He motioned to the pics.

Lake picked up the stack of photos and sat back in the chair at the same time. She went through them again, then looked to Sam and back down at the photos. "Sam, something doesn't look right about these."

She laid one of the most incriminating on the desk. "Do you have a magnifying glass?"

"Yeah, sure." He began rummaging around in the top desk drawer. "It's . . ." He shuffled through the top drawer. "Here."

"Thanks." She placed the square framed glass over the rocks. "Um . . . Okay, here, for instance. See the way the light looks coming from the left on the rocks over here? The shadows are cast slightly to the right . . . the angle . . . See?"

"Oh. Yeah . . . I see."

"Well, look at Elle. Notice anything strange?"

Sam's lips pressed a straight line. "Sorry, Lake. I don't."

"Look closer."

His concentrated frown deepened. "Hold on. Okay. What the—Elle doesn't have a shadow?"

Lake beamed. "Bingo. See what I mean? What kind of dog doesn't cast a shadow? A vampire dog?" With a negative shake of her head, Lake finished, "It wouldn't happen like this."

Sam's expression lightened and his shoulders relaxed a bit.

"They're faked? Are you sure? I mean, could it be a problem with the photo?"

"Umm. Looks like a consistent problem. They're all like that." She went through the stack with him this time. "I mean . . . Look, the light's coming from this direction—here. I'd need to enlarge them to be one hundred percent sure, but as it is, I'd say I'm ninety-nine and nine-tenths."

She thumbed through the rest of them. "Every one. Real issues. Inconsistencies." Lake frowned. "Yeah, I'm sure. I could enlarge them for you. I'm willing to bet that when they are—the manipulation should show up clearly."

Sam looked relieved. "Manipulated, huh? Can you do that for me?" Adding, "Can we document that?"

"Sure. Not a problem. Can you tell me what's going on?"

"Well, I'd rather not get into details, but it involves John Colter and Hawk . . . and Elle."

"Say no more. Do you want to do it right now?"

"Do you have time?"

"I'll make time." She smiled at him. "If someone's trying to pull a fast one on Elle—" she said Elle, but thought Hawk, too, "they'll need to try harder. C'mon."

The sheriff gathered the photos into a manila folder and they headed across the street to Lake's studio.

Two hours later, a relieved Sheriff Patrick held the evidence he needed in his hands. Proof that John Colter's photos of Elle, were faked. Big time.

"Whoever altered them, knew their way around Photoshop. Knew what they were doing, all right. If they hadn't made the mistake with the lighting on Elle, I might not have gone looking for the others. But they are there. All over the place, once you know to look. I've circled the areas on the copies with a Sharpie. Hawk might want to line up another expert, though."

Lake stretched and rubbed her neck, stiff from sitting still and staring for so long. She'd had enough practice to know the right spots to massage to relieve the tension.

Sam was off in another world. "Lake, I can't tell you how much this means to me. How much it will mean to Hawk. That dog is family to him." The sheriff's somber expression broke into a relieved smile. "You may have helped save a longstanding friendship too."

"Oh, come on. You two wouldn't have let this come between your friendship."

"I suppose not, but things didn't look too promising earlier. I need to let him know. He was ready to spit nails when he left. Excuse me."

Sam pulled out his phone and hit a number. She noticed he only hit one number—he must call Hawk a lot if he has him on speed dial. Sam waited, then shook his head.

"It's going to voicemail. Probably deliberate. I don't think he's too anxious to talk." Then, the recording must have started. "Hawk, listen. I've got news. Good news. We found inconsistencies with those photos. Looks like they're bogus. Call me ASAP."

"I'm sure, once Hawk sees these enlargements, it'll ease his mind."

Lake was pleased to see the sheriff's relief. And, well, she owed Hawk.

"Hawk might want to press some charges of his own." He patted the folder with the over-sized enlargements sticking out the ends. "Thanks again." He added still grinning. "And dinner tonight is definitely my treat. No arguments."

"Okay." She laughed. "I'll go for that. I need to drop River off for his class at the art center about six-thirty, so I should be at Suzanne's a few minutes after."

"Sounds good."

***

Lake watched Sam cross the street, then sat down to get some work done—but, somehow ended up considering how her efforts helping Sam might put a smile back on Hawk's face—and feeling more than good at the thought.

But, was it wise to let her thoughts travel that direction? Think girl, think. Was it smart? Hadn't she sworn off men—especially after Jeremy's true colors came through? After dating for a year, to have it end with a phone call. *"A six-year-old? You can't be seriously considering it. Tied down with a six-year-old?"* The words still rang in her ears as if Jeremy was standing next to her. *"Don't you have an aunt or someone –anyone—he could go to?"* Or, even worse, *"Aren't there lots of people waiting to adopt?"* He didn't have a clue. He hadn't even shown up for the memorial service—he was *on assignment*—although, by that time, she didn't want him there. Right. How could she have been so blind? Misjudged him so completely?

Note to self—ask more questions next time. Next time? Really? Would she ever be able trust her judgement again?

More to the point, how could she be attracted to another man so soon after the mess with Jeremy? And—face it—the little scene in Suzanne's cooler had clearly demonstrated what her subconscious felt about Hawk Matthews—no sense sailing down de-Nile.

Her thoughts ran on while her hands plaited her hair into her customary side braid. Six months since the crash. And to be fair, Hawk didn't seem like just another man. She *had* learned from the whole Jeremy experience, she was certain. But was it worth it? The chance of being hurt? Putting her heart out there again?

She was probably overthinking that kiss. Stop. Both she and Hawk were young, vital human beings of the opposite sex, in an emotionally super-charged situation—words were failing them. He probably regretted the whole thing happened.

To be honest, as a photographer, Lake knew the visual drew her attention. She'd let Jeremy's good looks hide the true man inside. Or maybe it wasn't hiding—maybe she hadn't been looking hard enough—purposely overlooking warning signs—avoidance of her family, his ambiguity toward faith.

Yeah, the warning flags were up, but she hadn't been paying attention.

She had stopped braiding. Shaking off the thoughts, she finished the braid, tying the end with a strip of leather, its ends decorated with dangling turquoise beads, that her parents had picked up in Santa Fe.

Her fingers closed around one of the shiny, blue beads. Turquoise—to the natives of the southwest—sky, water, bounty, security, protection.

With a sigh, she picked up one of the more promising photos, and tried to refocus on it. It worked—for a moment.

"The heart has its reasons of which reason knows nothing."

Unbidden, the Pascal quote floated through her mind, Hmm. Where had that come from? She hadn't thought of it since college.

Reason had to figure into everything she did now—she had a child to raise. She had to keep a clear head—reason—was essential.

It was getting harder to reason away Hawk Matthews. His serious nature ... his dark good-looks ... was she just rebounding from Jeremy's Scandinavian handsomeness?

Or something much more.

His words, "Straighten it out with *Him*, and leave me out of it," came back to her as clear as if he were standing right in front of her. A fire burned deep in the man's eyes. She'd had a glimpse of it then—and it was compelling. A light that came from inside. A light of truth.

Truth.

He'd confronted her with the truth in Suzanne's cooler—the truth of the motivation behind her hatred of him. A truth she had been determinedly avoiding—deliberately focusing her hatred on him to avoid her real issues.

There was much more to the man, so much more. She'd misjudged Hawk as wholly as she had misjudged Jeremy, but on a different level. Blasted by events of the past year, including Jeremy, she was more than willing to make Hawk a scapegoat.

Consciously or subconsciously, it didn't really matter. She'd slandered him all over town. How much pain had she inflicted on him? Lake groaned inwardly—almost physically sick remembering her comments.

She needed help. Lake closed her eyes in a simple prayer. *Help me set things right.*

Would she get the chance? Would she take the chance?

With a sigh, she turned back to the proofs on the table about the same time the phone rang—Casey Crawford, her editor. Just checking in on how *Timeframes* was progressing.

Lake shifted gears, pleased to tell her editor that the project was coming along, and should be wrapped up by the July eighteenth deadline. At least this part of her life was coming together. Once finished, fingers crossed, *Timeframes*, might give River and her breathing room financially. But that could be a year out yet and that was the best-case scenario.

They chatted for a couple more minutes, clarifying a few formatting issues. Satisfied, Casey said she's check back in a couple days. A busy woman, Casey was always direct, to the point. Lake appreciated that.

She missed talking to her in person, though. It was easier to work with people in person. Had she made the right decision in moving to Montana? Time would tell. River seemed to be adjusting. He loved animals and the outdoors and had his good buddy in Zach, his friend from church and school.

For that matter, Lake was discovering a dormant longing for the wilderness, that was springing to life with a little attention. Her parents found something here they could not forget. They'd spoken of returning to put permanent roots down and encouraged her to come along, but the draw of the city and its many distractions pulled her into its orbit.

Now, another world was drawing her in. A world which intuition was telling her, might be more fulfilling. Definitely worth investigating at any rate.

Her gaze drifted out the window and ran the length of white-capped lavender in the distance, settling on one particular mountain, and all its shadows. Could she find what she needed here? Would Harmony live up to its name?

Figuring out just what it was she needed would be a start.

Lake longed to get back out there. That morning, *before* the storm, had been thrilling. She'd never felt more alive. More grounded. A part of the earth and all its wonder.

With thoughts of wildness adventure bouncing around her head, Hawk's sign popped back into her mind. "*Sign up - wilderness survival class - community college.*"

Best heed the advice. With a phone call, a few minutes and a small dent to her checking account, Lake enrolled in "Wilderness Survival 101". Sounded fairly basic—just what she needed. Except for a few excursions with her parents, her photography experience was fairly an urban one. She looked through the open door to the storage room, its shelves packed with inherited camping equipment. The realization of how much she had counted on her parents to do prep work for outdoor shoots hit her.

Lake sighed. Hawk Matthews was right. She needed training. If she intended to complete her parents' tribute or follow in their footsteps, the class was more than a good idea, it could be a lifesaver.

Scheduled to meet on three consecutive Thursday evenings, the classes would be three hours each. Sounded do-able. Hmm. Maybe Fran or her son, Tyler could sit with River. The first class focused on a basic survival pack. What to include in it. How to signal for help. How not to get lost.

The second class, the registrar explained, covered keeping yourself in good condition if you did end up lost or stranded. There was a third class which was optional—an in the field, overnight excursion, to get hands on experience.

She was sure she would attend the first two, but she'd have to think about the third. That would be interesting. Overnight . . . She didn't know. If Fran could take River, perhaps she'd try to do that one, too.

That decided, she returned to the proofs and made some real headway. *"Timeframes"* was shaping up nicely, now that she had the missing camera back. The book would be a fitting tribute to her parents, she'd make sure of that.

Lost in choosing suitable shots for the book, the day flew by. Before she knew it, the bundle of energy named River came charging in the door after school.

"HiLakeheyguesswhat?"

When excited, River's sentences came out so fast they sounded like one continuous word. Lake looked up from her work, giving him full attention. His customary practice was to continue questioning, without giving her a chance to answer the last one. Most of the time, all she could do was watch him with an open-mouthed smile and raised eyebrows, nodding her interest as he raced on.

"You know my teacher, Miss James? She knows Ranger Randy." His jaw dropped open, displaying his amazement at the fact, then tumbled on, "Can you believe it Lake? She's good friends with him. He's gonna come to our school next week. The day before vacation. Can you believe it? It's gonna be sooo cooool."

River's excitement spilled out into the room like sunshine.

"Wow. That is exciting. Small world." Lake grinned. "Is he going to talk to you about animals or camping?" She barely got it out before he tumbled on.

"He is bringing animals with him. Can you believe it? This is going to be so cool. I can hardly wait."

It would be heaven on earth for River. His hero of the moment was Ranger Randy. "What kinds of animals?"

"They're not telling. It's a surprise." River's eyes lit up. "But I'm hoping he brings a real, live wolf. Oh man, that would be sooo awesome!"

"That would be awesome." Lake's eyes sparkled back at his. It was so good to see him with his light turned on again. The first couple months after the accident, well, she wondered if it would ever happen.

"You know what else would be awesome?" Lake widened her eyes as she asked.

"What?"

"If you would go change into that old shirt you save for painting. The green striped one with the blue paint on it—from when we painted your room. I have a feeling it'll get messy tonight. I'll finish up my work here then I'll warm up the goulash. Do you have any homework?"

"Just my spelling list."

"Okay. Good. We'll spend a few minutes on that before you eat. I'm going to meet Sheriff Sam at Suzanne's for supper tonight while you're at your art lesson."

Alarm washed over River's face. "Sheriff Sam? Is something wrong—that you're meeting Sheriff Sam, I mean?" His brow crinkled with worry.

"Oh, no. No. Nothing like that. I helped him out with some pictures today and he offered to buy me supper. We're friends. He's a nice guy. I like him. Kind of makes me think of what having a big brother would be like." She tilted her head and gazed into the distance, smiling broadly at the mental image.

River glanced up quick as a shot. "Would you rather have a big brother instead of a little one?"

"Oh, Riv . . ." She picked him up from under his arms and swung him around in two big circles speaking as they spun. "Neeeevvvvrrrr. Why would you ask such a thing? If they offered me my choice of a million, no, a *billion, trillion, gazillion* other brothers, I would always choose you."

River giggled.

"You're one in a *gazillion*." She laughed.

A couple more swings around the room and a couple of hoots later, River wriggled away, his face flushed from fun. He looked out the big windows, a realization hitting him.

"Laa-aake. Stop! The guys might see. You know, I'm not a *baby* anymore."

"Oh, right." Lake tugged the bill of his blue Chicago Cubs cap down over his eyes. "Well, *Mr.* McDonald, you'd better go change and let me finish here. I'll be up soon."

River took the stairs at full speed as he ran up to the apartment. He *was* one in a gazillion and she would be lost without him.

When a shocked forty-year-old Anne McDonald confirmed her queasy feeling was the second child they had hoped for years to have, but never been blessed with, she had called him a gift from God. And that was the middle name she and Caleb gave River—Matthew—*Gift from God.*

And what would Lake have done without the gift of River? He was a gift. Lake spent the next few minutes solemnly pondering the twists and turns life can take, busying her hands with tidying up the worktable. Would she ever understand?

One truth she did know, she and River would be lost without each other right now.

"La-ake. My paint shirts gone. It's not nowhere." Came a call from the top of the stairs.

"It's not *any*where, River."

"I know. What should I wear?"

"Under the jeans, middle drawer." She called over her shoulder, smiling at his wording and notorious disorganization. Organization would come in time. Lake could barely manage to keep two shoes in the same room when she was six.

Well, admittedly, the shoe problem hadn't improved that much.

A couple minutes later, the call came from upstairs. Crisis averted. "It's okay. I found it."

***

Paint shirt found, spelling words studied, supper eaten, and River dropped off at the art center at twenty after six, put Lake ahead of schedule and ready to relax. More than enough time to drive to the café, but it really didn't make sense to go home. Maybe she should drop the jeep off at the apartment and walk. But it would be almost dark when River got out of his class and he would be tired. She drove straight to the café, parked the jeep and then parked herself in a booth by a front window, adjusting the shade a bit to block the slanted evening sunlight.

Suzanne was headed her direction, looking pleased with herself.

"I made an addition to the menu." She handed one to Lake, with a flourish, "Just for you." Her dangling turquoise earrings bobbed as she nodded toward the menu on the red tabletop. "Check out the *beverages*."

Lake scanned the columns on the cheerful menu, decorated with yellow-breasted, black-tied Western Meadowlarks, Montana's state bird, and little pink Bitterroot flowers, the state flower. Now that she was back, Suzanne was enthusiastic about promoting her home state. There, under Hot Beverages was, *Lake's Spiced Chai*.

"Cool. My chai. I'm famous." Suzanne had been mixing up her special chai brew especially for her the past few months.

"You were already famous, honey. You have a whole, big lake named after you." Suz winked at her reversal of the facts. "But I had *so* many people asking what that terrific smell was, I had to add it—by popular demand—you might say. It's been going over great, too." She nodded at a couple in the corner and added, "Adds a bit of *international* flavor to the place." She held up an imaginary teacup with her pinkie out and winked. "Thanks for sharing your recipe, by the way."

"Oh, absolutely."

"Hey Lake. Hey Suzanne." Sam deposited his Stetson on the post beside the booth and sat down across from Lake.

"I'll give you two a couple of minutes to decide." Suzanne chirped and went to another table.

Conversation quickly found its way back to the faked photos.

"What did Hawk have to say when you told him?" Lake couldn't contain her curiosity any longer.

"Hasn't gotten back to me yet." Sam frowned and shook his head. "It's not like him. He's always got that phone on for GRRR calls." He raised his eyebrows. "Which means, he's still ticked. Can't say I blame him. Colter put me in a heck of a position . . . and the more I think about it, the more I think he knew exactly what he was doing."

"Hey, I'm sure everything will be all right. You guys have been friends forever—didn't you say that?"

"Yeah, since high school football."

Suzanne's return to take their orders redirected their attention back to the menus, and Lake made sure to steer conversation away from Hawk for the rest of dinner—which took a surprising bit of effort on her part.

SEVEN

Art Lesson

Funny thing, but Hawk couldn't have explained *why* he looked up when he did, but when he did, Lake was making her way into the classroom. Even through all the chattering and commotion, her *vibe* came through. Like it or not, his internal radar was set on Lake McDonald frequency.

He found himself headed in her direction without making a conscious decision to do so. She saw him coming and—smiled. A *stunning* smile. A—knock-the-boots-off-the-cowboy—smile. It caused a catch in his step. *Whoa.* He swallowed hard. *Get a grip Matthews.* What are you—seventeen?

What had he done to deserve a smile like that from her? Had she taken his words to heart? Whatever it was, he would have to figure it out and keep doing it. A guy could go weak in the knees from a smile like that. Genuine, unpretentious. No woman's smile had ever done that to him. It was a bit daunting.

Too bad the smile wasn't directed at him.

Still smile-struck, Hawk was almost bowled over from behind as River hurtled by him at full speed toward Lake. He watched as she hugged him warmly and realized the smile that had knocked him off the mountain was really aimed at her little brother, charging forward from the back of the room. His own smile twisted a little sideways attempting to hide his chagrin. That was one lucky kid. Obviously a very loved kid.

Mesmerized, Hawk watched her nod and smile, examining River's creation in the shoe box. A touching scene. The two had the same rich, dark-chocolate hair color—the same vivid blue eyes. Angular jaw lines. The same *spunk*. The boy could be a miniature, masculine version of Lake.

Right about then, she did turn her eyes to his.

Realizing his expression had turned serious, Hawk pasted a welcoming smile back on his face and nodded. She returned his smile—a smile that did not reach her eyes. Confusion? Regret about the cooler episode?

He mentally kicked himself again for letting his emotions get away from him the other day. Lake looked as skittish as a colt and ready to bolt. He'd have to be cool, reassure her. No pressure.

Hawk reined in his thoughts and resumed his path toward them. On the way, he was accosted by two students and their respective parents. In the brief amount of time it took to exchange greetings and encouragements about their creative talents, Lake and River had disappeared from the room.

***

On the ride home, River inspected his creation, while Lake replayed the classroom scene in her head. She'd examined River's sculpture, giving herself as much time as possible to determine what it was. She could tell by the four legs it was some kind of animal, but she had to rev up her imagination to come up with the *right* animal.

At her, "Hey Riv! What 'cha got there?"

River uncovered his treasure proudly with a, "Look Lake. Isn't it great?"

She'd knelt beside him to get a better look and wrapped her arm around him. Good to see him so involved and happy. She'd given him a little squeeze, but not too much. She didn't want to embarrass him. *He wasn't a baby anymore*, she reminded herself with a smile.

He'd lifted the shoebox at her. "Rooo-aarr!"

Ah, the clue she needed. "Wow, Riv. Your . . . bear looks like it could almost walk right out of that box."

Bingo. Relief. According to his huge smile, she'd guessed correctly.

"I would have rather done a wolf, but Hawk said that bears are easier to start with. Hawk's really cool. You *have* to meet him. He makes animals and stuff for his work. It's what he does all day. Isn't that cool? He said my bear has good fur. He said I have real po-ten-shell. What's po-ten-shell, Lake? Where is he? You have to meet him . . . Oh. There he is. He's coming this way." Then River had grabbed his big sister's hand to pull him toward Hawk—but she was stronger.

Mercifully, a few other children and parents stopped their popular instructor to talk.

***

What had happened? Why the sudden attack of shyness? Why had she run? It shouldn't have surprised her that Hawk was teaching the sculpting class. The art center said they used local artists and evidently, from the way the children were responding, he had a way with them.

After the long winter and *never* running into Hawk Matthews, were their paths now to intersect at every turn? Although, she had to admit, she had isolated herself for much of the fall and winter. She didn't feel ready to do small-talk with him in such a public setting, yet.

They had both done a kindness for the other, he found and returned her camera, and she, helped Sam determine the photos were faked.

But she didn't have the right words for him yet. What *were* the right words? She sighed. No clue.

At least River enjoyed himself and tonight's art lesson. Hawk had facilitated that. He deserved the credit. River was happy. That's all that really mattered.

At least that's what she kept telling herself.

Granted, Hawk Matthews was one good-looking man—and she had met a lot of good-looking men. Some of those models—well, a girl had to work to keep her mouth from dropping open. But, she had learned the hard way, it took more than looks to make a man of substance.

What was she doing harboring her thoughts in this port anyway? Hadn't she decided to sail any ideas like those directly back out to sea after the whole thing with Jeremy? She had nearly drowned in her delusions about him. What was wrong with her? Had she learned nothing? How much did she really know about Hawk? Her heart might skip a beat, or pound out an extra one, but she had to keep her feet planted firmly on shore. Think. She couldn't go through that again—for her sake *and* River's. They needed stability and honesty and trust.

All things she was evidently unable to recognize in a man—or maybe didn't know to look for before . . .

Even if Hawk was all he appeared to be—she had to acknowledge the eight-hundred-pound gorilla in the room—Hawk's work with GRRR was dangerous—life-threatening dangerous. As in—be ripped away from those you love without warning, dangerous.

And there it was.

Lake stared at the road. Her internal vision cleared. There it was. Loving and losing. Life was so fragile. Why deliberately pour yourself into a relationship that could be torn away at a moment's notice—to someone trying to fix someone's else's disaster?

Didn't River need more than that? Didn't *she* deserve better than chancing a tidal wave like that knocking her down again?

Someday, when River was grown, maybe she'd be more open to the possibility, but not now. It was too much to figure out.

No matter how many ruggedly handsome mountain men crossed her path.

". . . and Hawk said to keep the wet cloth over the clay, but Zach forgot and his clay got all crumbly and stuff, but it was okay because Hawk got him some more clay and . . . Lake . . . Lake?"

She realized River had been talking to her. *See?* she told herself, *your attention is being drawn away from where it is supposed to be. Get with it.*

"Sorry. Zach's clay got crumbly?"

"Yeah, but Hawk fixed it. And then Zach got his bear made too. But I like mine better."

"I like yours too, because you made it special. But you know what? I bet Zach and his mom like his project a lot too, because it's something special he made himself. What do you think?"

"That's kinda what Hawk said. He said everyone makes their own kinds of art. It's all you-neek. That means special. Right?"

"That's right Riv. Just like you." She reached over and tousled his hair. "You-neek." She had to give Hawk credit for making that point clear to the kids.

"Hawk's really cool, Lake. Did I tell you that?"

"Ahh . . . Yes, hon. You did mention it a couple of times."

"Oh, yeah. Well, I think it's too bad so many people wanted to talk to him and we had to go so fast. I wish you could have met him."

"Actually, I have met him."

"You have? You didn't tell me. When? Isn't he cool? You know he makes sculptures every day? For his work. He's a sculpture-maker, all the time."

"He's a sculptor. Sculp-tor."

"That's what I *said*. *I* didn't know you guys *knew* each other. You guys . . . *already* know each other? We should ask him over for supper."

"I know him—just a little bit," she answered softly.

He had been so anxious for her to talk to Hawk, she felt a little guilty for avoiding it. Thankfully, they were home and the conversation turned to being careful with the box.

The next morning, her guilt about dragging River off so quickly the night before still lingered. She didn't know how to deal with Hawk just yet. But, the vision of him standing there, smiling at her and at all those little children clamoring around him—well, it undid her. She couldn't have found words then anyway.

The big talk she had given herself about being careful? Not letting herself get involved? What a joke. She had no more than laid eyes on Hawk last night—had no more than one devastating smile from him—and she was mentally right back in his arms.

This wouldn't do. Couldn't do. She had to get a better handle on her emotions. But where to start? She wasn't ready. How could Hawk look so cool?

***

The next couple of weeks passed uneventfully. Was that good or bad? With emotions still waging war within her, maybe it was good. At least she got some quality work done.

But, truth be told, she was a little disappointed she hadn't seen a certain rugged sculptor around town. It wasn't for lack of scanning the street every time she went out. Lake shook her head. Foolish.

The weather had turned cloudy and chilly again, making it easier to focus attention on winding up "*Timeframes*" without being lured outside. Casey called a couple of times about some issues and they discussed the forward for the book. Casey wanted her to write it. Have the daughter's perspective. It made sense, but Lake was no writer and it would take her some time. Of course, Casey was right on this. It was appropriate. She'd be proud to do it—but how to compress all her thoughts and feelings about her parents into a few pages?

She was trained in the art of, "a picture is worth a thousand words", not the other way around.

With that thought, an idea formed . . . perhaps she could do a sort of narrated family album at the beginning of the book, through a few family pictures. Let those say the thousands of words for the most part. Lake would work on that angle. Casey agreed.

Then there was marketing. Yikes. They discussed promotion of the book once it was in print, probably early summer of next year. That would be good timing. Summer would be easier to arrange. Riv could come with.

The fact that River was in the picture, and the fact that neither them had been on a plane since . . . well . . . travel would be a little trickier. At least there was time. The idea of getting on a plane again, for either of them, would take some time to wrap their heads around. How would River react to the idea? She might need professional advice on this one.

Yes, it would certainly take more advanced planning. Not her strong point.

She was used to deadlines, of course, but she had always pretty much had the freedom of jumping in the jeep or on a plane when inspiration struck. Now she realized what a luxury that had been.

She wouldn't trade River for any amount of convenience her single life had offered. His love and care, no matter how difficult at times to fit into her life, was a blessing, and she would never allow herself to forget it. Her mind echoed with the sound of his busy footsteps up and down the stairs at the back of the studio . . . his laughter . . . his contagious enthusiasm.

A fantasy skipped its way through Lake's head about what it would have been like to have a bigger family—more brothers and sisters, but, it wasn't meant to be.

Her thoughts strayed into the family area more and more lately. Only natural, she supposed, considering what had happened. What she was missing.

Lake tapped the eraser of the yellow, wooden pencil on her lips as her gaze drifted out the studio window. Children of her own . . . In her mind's eye, a hazy scene swirled past, with children around a table . . . two . . . three . . . four . . .

What?! She blinked hard. Where had that come from?

Funny thing was, when dating Jeremy, those kinds of thoughts never entered her mind. Why not? They'd dated for over a year, but neither had ever even broached the subject of what they envisioned.

Looking back, had they really talked about anything that mattered to building a quality life? Except work. They were both passionate about their work.

She supposed the death of her parents and River's full-time entrance into her life triggered all the—what am I doing with my life—thoughts. Only natural. But, the thought of a roomful of children appealing to her? Huh, who'd have thought.

With a jolt, Lake realized she'd been staring in the direction of Shadow Mountain. Blinking herself back to reality, she couldn't ignore the lingering question. Could she find an answer there?

Trouble was, it took two to make the little daydream developing in her mind's eye happen in real the real world.

Frowning, she popped the thought bubble with a vengeance.

EIGHT

It's All Coming Back

Before Lake knew it, the day rolled around for her first survival class. Fran had enthusiastically endorsed the idea and volunteered for sitter duty.

"Now there's a smart idea." she approved with gusto. "I'm glad *Hawk Matthews* suggested it."

Lake narrowed a look at Fran and the extra zing she added to his name.

"Considerate of him to show an interest—don't you think?" she pressed on.

Lake's outdoor skills might not be the best, but she recognized a fishing expedition and wasn't about to bite.

"I'm sure he is trying to avoid a future emergency call for the GRRR squad. Doesn't want to have to scrape me off the bottom of a ravine, or chip me out of a snowbank somewhere," Lake continued, as she stuffed a small notebook and pen in her over-sized leather shoulder-bag.

"I'm sure he wouldn't want to do that. The question is, what *does* he want to do with you?"

"Fran. Really. Stop. It's nothing like that. Believe me." Lake inserted extra emphasis and a frown to her denial and with a shake of her head added, "He's just trying to help."

She pulled on the fitted blue jacket that matched her eyes, pretending to ignore the fact that Fran was smiling like the Cheshire cat.

Thankfully, River was oblivious to Fran's innuendos.

"Do you have to take anything with you?" River chimed in. "Like a backpack, or notebook, or anything?" His interest in the class was bubbling over, and was disappointed he couldn't go along, but seemed satisfied with her assurance that she would teach him all she learned and promised to look for a wilderness class for his age group.

"No, Riv—just a notebook and pen tonight. All in here." She patted her bag and slung it over her shoulder, then bent to give River a hug.

"You have fun with Fran, but remember," she looked at him seriously, "pajamas on by eight-thirty and bed at nine."

"Aw, can't I stay up 'til you get home? I could practice my reading."

"You know the answer to that, but nice try you little conniver." She ruffled the hair on his head as he gave a guilty grin. "I shouldn't be too late. I'll come and tuck in your covers when I get back." She gave them a quick smile as she pulled the door shut.

***

Six fifty-three. The class was scheduled to start at seven p.m. She nodded and smiled to the other students she passed on her way to a desk at the back. Her spot. The best place to observe the scene. The best place to get the angles, the right shots. Force of habit.

Well, that was part of it. The other was a natural tendency. She was not the one to pick if you needed a parade led, or a rally run. No, she was much more comfortable behind the scenes, getting the big picture . . . considering all the angles.

She checked her watch again. Five to. From the looks of it, there were about a dozen people attending.

An older couple, four athletic, twenty-something guys, who appeared to know each other from the way they were talking and laughing, three women sitting right in front of her—two looked to be in their twenties and one probably late thirties, a teenage boy and herself.

A gray-haired gentleman in a slightly crumpled khaki shirt, probably the instructor, entered the room and walked to the desk. Huh, a little older than she would have expected, but he probably had loads of experience in the back country. Nothing like having lived what you were teaching. Lake settled into learning mode, focusing on the instructor. She watched as he placed items on the desk . . . a small mirror, a few feet of rolled up twine, a light stick, a . . .

Funny, he seemed uncomfortable as he looked around. Why? As his glance met hers, she smiled and he smiled back. Was she wrong? Was he new? She doubted it.

The sound of the door opening drew his attention and put a relieved grin on his face. "Oh, there you are. Thank heavens. I thought I was going to have to start teaching the class myself."

Lake leaned back in her chair and a did a double-take as Hawk and Elle enter the room.

Oh, boy.

After signaling the dog to lie down beside the podium, Hawk gave a brief glance around the room. Had he noticed her react? Be cool.

"Had a GRRR call this afternoon, Ed. Sorry to make you nervous, but I figured I'd make it on time if I hurried. And look, we're here, one minute to spare." He patted Ed on the back.

Ed's relief was apparent. "Good-timing. I'll just get out of your way then. Have a good class." The older man gave Elle a pet on his way out of the room.

"Thanks Ed."

Hawk turned to his students.

"Hello everyone." He glanced around. "I do know most of you, but for the rest, I'm Hawk Matthews. I grew up around here and for the past twelve years I've been privileged to work with Glacier Rescue Rapid Response. Please, call me Hawk." He reached down and scratched the wolfish dog behind the ears. "And this is Elle, short for Cinderella."

At the curious glances, he continued with a smile and pat on the shoulder for Elle.

"I was fortunate enough to adopt her after the West Slope fire five years ago. She was a pup and covered in ash—all cinders and soot when we found her wandering out of a hot-spot. But, she's a survivor. Aren't you girl?" He patted her flank. "We searched everywhere we could think of for her owner, but nothing, so I adopted her. A few burns, but she recovered nicely. She's family now . . . and a great asset. Great nose—tracks beautifully. Sociable too, in case any of you want to make her acquaintance after class."

As if on cue, Elle sat up and raised a furry paw to shake, followed by a round of "Aws", from the class.

Hawk straightened up from returning the shake, smiled and started, "Okay. I'll be your guide for the next three weeks as we talk about respect for nature."

There were a few frowns.

"Oh, right. You thought this was a survival class." Lake was glad she was sitting as Hawk flashed a smile her direction. "Right. It is. First lesson—big—important—lesson. Respect nature. It's not referred to as the power of nature for nothing. We are bit players in a huge system. It can be beautiful. It can be inspiring. It can be deadly. Never forget that."

Well, he certainly commanded the attention of the room, she'd give him that. The formerly rowdy guys were paying close attention and the women, well the women could only be described as transfixed. Not a major surprise, she supposed, since their instructor looked like he'd just stepped out of GQ on his way to an Iron Man triathlon.

She smiled at their reaction, then noted, her own eyes seemed to be glued overlong to the GRRR logo on the front of the sage green t-shirt stretched across the well-defined musculature of his chest. Must lift weights. He wasn't muscle-bound, but you could tell the man worked out. She continued the appreciation of this fact as her eyes traveled to his biceps, then back to his eyes which were—which were looking straight into hers.

Busted. She looked down and grabbed for the hand-book on her desk, deftly knocking it to the floor with a slap. All heads turned toward her. *Sugar.* She retrieved it, but couldn't help but note Hawk's amused expression when she was brave enough to look up again. She hoped she'd masked her startled expression in time. Had he caught her appraisal of his physique? *Double sugar.* He might get the wrong impression—or—the right one? Arrrgh.

The trace of a smile still evident, Hawk cleared his throat and continued, "First of all, I want to thank you for coming, for taking the time to protect yourselves and take charge of your own survival. One of the most important things I've learned in the past twelve years of my involvement with GRRR, is that the people who do *not* view themselves as victims, who are informed, active participants in their survival are much more likely to do just that. Survive."

"Second, I want to personally thank all of you for becoming informed, which will lessen the chances of Elle and me having to leave our warm cabin in the middle of the night to pull your sorry butts out of some jam you've gotten yourselves into out there—stuck in a tree, or on the side of a sheer cliff, or on a log about to go over Harmony Falls, or turning yourselves into human popsicles, or Smokey the Bear's supper, or whatever other creative ways people seem to keep coming up with. Granted, life-threatening situations happen that cannot be avoided, but we are here to talk about the ones that can be."

Lake wondered what you would call his voice. Clear and strong. Baritone? Tenors were higher, weren't they? Hmmm. Did he do any singing? The church had a choir but it sang at ten-thirty and she'd been taking River to the service and Sunday school at nine. Sam mentioned Hawk went there too. How their conversation had traveled there, she didn't remember, but you'd think with a voice like that it would sound good singing. She forced her attention away from the sound of his voice back to the content...

"So, tonight we will talk about pretty basic stuff. Simple-basic-stuff. Not glamorous, but effective. The first is a little thing I like to call—the plan. Many people, who shall remain nameless—except for those who end up as front-page fodder—start their wilderness trips with little more than a spirit of enthusiasm."

Lake managed to keep her jaw from dropping as he focused on her in a silent exchange—which his eyes and expression said—*this means you.* Mercifully, his gaze traveled on before the full effects of her blush hit.

Cool down, Lake. You know he's right.

"*The plan* involves looking at a map, doing research on the area you'll be traveling, and, this is a big one, pay attention people—letting someone know exactly *where* you are going, *what* time you are leaving and *what time* you expect to be back. Super important. I can't emphasize this enough. If more people would use "the plan" technique of wildness excursion, our calls at GRRR would probably be cut in half. No kidding . . . in half." He topped off this fact with an intense look around the room.

"So—okay. Let's say you're on your hike, full of enthusiasm, out there appreciating all the good things the Creator has provided and you get lost in the moment . . . become literally lost, or heaven forbid . . . you trip over a rock while in amazement at how tall the trees really are and break a leg."

He looked up at the ceiling and raised his hands and eyebrows in mock awe at this point, bringing a chuckle from the class. "If people know where you are headed, there will be people looking for you when you don't show up when you were expected. That is—if you used 'the plan'".

The pretty blond flashed a sideways smile at the brunette and whispered loudly, "I'm making a plan right now to get lost, if he's the one who's gonna come find me."

"Maybe you'll get lucky and be on call nurse for a GRRR rescue flight with him," the brunette whispered back.

Oh, they're nurses, thought Lake, as the full effect of their conversation took hold of her. Rescue flight . . . Rescue flights? Hawk Matthews goes on rescue . . . *flights*. Of course he did. Small planes. Lake's stomach did a serious turn. Her palms were getting sweaty. Rescue flights . . . small planes . . . How could she forget the fact? Why had she only pictured Hawk Matthews on ropes and backpack kinds of rescues? She took a shaky breath.

Small planes . . .

Somewhere in the background, Lake was aware of Hawk's voice . . . something about a compass, a mirror . . . light stick . . . with you. But the brunette nurse's whispered comment had thrown her for a loop.

GRRR rescue flights . . . Lake was unprepared for the onslaught of emotion . . . the memory of that fateful telephone call . . . flight down . . . your parents flight . . . jarring images of emergency vehicle lights flashed through her mind—and the sound of newscasts: "World-renowned photographer couple's flight downed by freak blizzard."

The classroom dimmed from view, and, like rows of dominos tumbling over, memories clattered to the front of her consciousness, vivid as the awful day they'd happened. Even worse, the memories continued tumbling, to three days later when the weather cleared as first, the broken wings were discovered, followed, a short-time later, by the crumpled pile of metal that had been the fuselage. The memory of Fran's hands trying unsuccessfully to hold her back from seeing the aerial reports of the crash scene on television . . . trying to keep her from seeing . . . seeing what she never should have seen. No child, whatever age, should see their parents . . . like that.

Through bleary eyes Lake fought to clear her focus. *God help me, I'm losing it.* Where was this coming from? She hadn't had an episode for months. Vaguely aware her hands were shaking, she fumbled for her purse. Tried to calm herself. She looked to the front of the room and through the fog, registered the concerned expression pointed at her from Hawk.

What is going on? Why is this happening again? Now? Get it together.

She had to get out of there. Get home.

Heart pounding, her eyes darted to the door. Could she slip out without making a scene? A quick glance around evidenced it was too late for that. She grabbed onto her bag and started down the aisle, stumbling a bit over the brunette's purse on the floor.

"Sorry. Oh, sorry," she mumbled, head down on her way past the desks and curious glances. "Something I ate," Lake fibbed and bumped her way to the front of the room.

Don't look up. Don't look at him. She saw Hawk's legs move to stand from his sitting position on the desk, but knew she couldn't face any questions. She couldn't meet anyone's eyes right now.

Why had the words *rescue flight* hit her like that? Now, after all this time, had they triggered the onslaught of vivid, painful memories? She must have heard the word *flight* hundreds of times since the accident. Why tonight? Why now?

Mouth dry, heart pounding, Lake felt she'd run the length of a football field as she made for the goal line—the door.

Still trying to catch her breath, Lake was in the hall, rounding the corner headed for the parking lot, when a voice from behind stopped her.

"Lake. Wait. Slow down . . . *Wait a minute.*" Hawk's compelling voice broke through the fog.

Her forward motion slowed to almost a stop, but she couldn't force herself to turn. A warm, firm grip on her shoulders did it for her. Chancing a glance up at Hawk, she was reassured by the compassion she found there. Had she ever felt this embarrassed? But no, it was more than that. More like—vulnerable—in her life?

"Come. Here. Sit." He motioned to a bench along the side of the hallway and gently maneuvered her there without waiting for a reply. "Give yourself a minute. Sit down—before you fall down."

It was good to sit, but not as good as the strong arm wrapped around her and the hand rubbing her upper arm in support. After what was probably only a minute, but seemed like an eternity, Lake's breathing settled to near normal, and her pulse slowed considerably.

She tried to shove the plane crash memories as far back in her mind as she could.

"I'm . . . sorry." Lake managed another look at Hawk. His look of concern disarmed her. But it wasn't a bad feeling. It reassured her. She wanted to be able to trust him.

Wanted to dive into that feeling. She frowned at the revelation.

"I... Don't you need to be in class? They'll revolt soon... demand refunds."

Back in control now, Lake attempted to lighten the mood.

Hawk's look was tender. He wasn't put off course by her tactic to get rid of him. "We're taking a break. We take two breaks a class anyway. So what if this one's a little ahead of schedule. Besides, they're grown-ups, they'll be okay." Then he continued, "So, does the PTSD hit often?"

"What?"

"The PTSD... Post-Traumatic Stress Disorder. Does it hit often??"

Lake focused on the furrow of concern between his dark brows as she tried to decide how to answer.

"Well—I," she trailed off. It would be futile to try and explain away a reaction he obviously recognized.

He continued when she hesitated, "At first I thought you were surprised, put off maybe, that I was teaching the class and didn't tell you. Of course, I knew there was a class coming up." He said it with a little apologetic grin. "I would have told you, but I thought you wouldn't come. The *idea,* well, beside the fact you do need the training, was to show you that I'm not such a bad guy." There was that dimple again. "But when I saw the level of your reaction, well, I figured there's something else. You know Lake, I've seen plenty of PTSD, and I'm wondering if that's what's going on with you—or a panic attack. The question is, *why*? What triggered it? Was it something I said?"

Lake stared at the opposite wall. No sense in trying to hide it. Nothing to be embarrassed about—right? That's what the therapist had told her. She kept her eyes on the wall and said quietly, "The first three months after seeing the accident scene on TV were the worst. I went to some therapy sessions. It helped. I thought they were gone. It's been months—until tonight." She spoke the words, mostly to herself.

The heat of Hawk's comforting hand seeped into Lake's consciousness and she glanced at the lean, strong fingers wrapped around her arm. At her look, he removed his hand, but the warmth lingered and Lake wished he hadn't misinterpreted her look as one of discomfort.

Goose bumps replaced the warmth and she wrapped her arms around herself. Was she so starved for a man's touch? Or *this* man's touch? They definitely had chemistry, as evidenced at Suzanne's. But chemistry could get you into trouble. Her feelings were so all over the place right now. The last thing she needed in her life right now was man drama. Right? She had River to look out for. Right. Of course, that was right. The thought shook her back to reality.

But Hawk did deserve an explanation.

"I'm almost afraid to say it now," she frowned at let out a nervous laugh. "Flight," she stated flatly, turning her face to his as she spoke the trigger word. "Rescue flight." She looked down at her lap. Her hands had steadied. "Those—they must have been nurses, I think—in front of me (he nodded affirmatively to this) were talking about you and rescue flights." She shook her head in disbelief, "I can't believe it hit me like that—kind of knocked me for a loop. It's been months," she added, her voice apologetic.

"Sure." He looked at the opposite wall, considering. "That could trigger it. Make's sense."

"How'd you know about my PTSD?"

"We're trained to watch for it in the squad. And, well, Sam mentioned you told him about it."

Lake sent him a questioning look.

"Yeah . . . uh . . . guilty. I asked about you. Does that bother you—that I was pushing Sam for information, I mean?"

Lake wasn't sure how she should answer that. Honestly, she was finding him more attractive all the time and she doubted if there was a woman alive who wouldn't be flattered by his attention, but should she let on, before she really knew more about him? Her judgment in men had fallen far short in the past. She didn't trust herself anymore.

After River's full-time appearance into and Jeremy's disappearance out of, her life just a few months earlier, hadn't she vowed to steer clear of men? Could Hawk be different? He seemed to understand what she was going through. And, after the terrible way she had treated him, slandered him, he still seemed willing to . . . to what?

She'd be honest, but evasive.

"I don't really know why you would ask Sam about me. The way I treated you . . . the things I said . . ." She blinked. "What do you think I should think about it?"

Hawk half-smiled and put his hand back on her shoulder. He lowered his head. "You know," he sighed, "I've been going through some stuff. I haven't handled things the best myself, lately. I'm hoping we can start over. Not judge by first . . . or second impressions." He winced. "I'll be honest, Lake. I'd like to get to know you." The topaz eyes searched her face. "I know you've had a lot to cope with. I'm sorry. PTSD is understandable after a trauma like you've been through." His look was sympathetic. "But I was kind of hoping that we could spend some time together. I could show you the country around here." Then, he grinned. "After all, it does seem you could use a good guide."

The grin was contagious.

"I could use a good guide—and a good friend."

It couldn't hurt to get to know him better. She'd be careful. Take it slow. Her calm returned, for the most part.

"Listen, I think I'm good now. You better get back to your students. They'll be demanding a refund." She smiled to reinforce her claim.

His eyes, still warm with concern, were trained on her. His head tilted. "You're sure you're feeling okay?"

"Yes. Yes, I'm fine. Embarrassed—but much better."

"Nothing to be embarrassed about. You're coming back in?"

"You know, I think I need a little time to sort this out." Lake gave a weak smile. "But, if you wouldn't mind, my email is on my registration. Could you email me the information from tonight? If it's not too much trouble, I mean—I'd really appreciate it."

"Listen Lake, I can do better than that. Maybe this isn't the best setting for you. I owe you—I still feel bad about how rude I was to you when Elle was hit and I especially owe you for working with Sam on those faked photos." He pressed his lips together, considering. It made a dimple show. "Let me make it up to you by repeating the lesson for you in person."

Her heart beat faster as his comforting voice wrapped around her like a warm, soft blanket. She swallowed hard and shook the errant thought away, focusing on his suggestion, turning her eyes to his. "Oh, I don't want you to go to a lot of trouble. Sam says you have an awful lot on your plate."

Shoot. That slipped out. She didn't really want to let Hawk know they had been discussing him. He might get the idea, the *correct* idea, she thought with chagrin, of just how interested she was. Better to figure out her jumble of emotions toward him before she telegraphed too much. But she could tell by the fleeting expression that passed over his face, he was sharp enough to catch on.

"Seems like Sam's been answering a lot of questions," He grinned, adding "from both directions—and it's no trouble.

Believe me, I feel like a real heel about the way I acted. Let me make it up to you."

"I don't know . . ."

"You can bring River, if you like." He prompted. "At the sculpture class, River expressed quite an interest in the outdoors."

"Hawk, is everything okay out here? Will class be starting again soon?" The older brunette nurse interrupted Lake as her head poked out from around the corner.

Lake's whisper took a more serious tone, "I told you. The revolt is starting."

He smiled enough to make the other dimple appear too. "I'll be right in, Cathy." Then to Lake, "You okay to drive?" He asked and wrapped his fingers around her wrist, feeling her pulse. "Your pulse is still going a pretty good clip."

No surprise there. It would be, as long as he was holding her wrist. At her affirmative nod, he got up. "Okay. I'll call you tomorrow. We can discuss the details of your wilderness training. You're sure you're okay to drive?"

She nodded her assurance and thanked him, watching as he rejoined the nurse and they re-entered the classroom.

Lake stayed on the bench for a couple more minutes, making sure she'd recovered from the episode—and, admit it—the effects of being near Hawk again.

What was she thinking? She dug in her bag for her keys and headed for the jeep.

A few minutes in his company and she was already stomping all over her best intentions to stay away from men.

How could she even consider spending more time around him? With each encounter, she could feel her resolve crumbling a bit more.

Hopeless endeavor. He might be the most attractive man in the world, might prove himself to be trustworthy and honest, to give River a chance, but there was still a huge roadblock with all kinds of warning signs flashing. From where she stood now, Lake saw no way around it. The man went up in small rescue planes for heaven's sake—in ferocious weather and placed himself in dicey situations. How could she even consider putting herself through that, over and over? Still, the pull was there, like iron to a magnet. He would be a great friend to have. Could she keep any other emerging feelings in check?

Did she want to?

***

Hawk refocused on teaching the rest of his class that evening. He was good at compartmentalizing what needed to be done. It was one skill you developed quickly when working search and rescue—no distractions. Focus. Keep your head in the game. Whatever else is going on in your life will be there later.

Lately, he found himself wanting to deal with Lake McDonald a lot more.

So, it was no surprise that on the drive back to Shadowhawk that night, his thoughts circled round to her again.

Man—watch yourself. He'd have to tread fast to keep his head above water when it came to Lake McDonald. As for her, life had swept a wave of disaster over her family and she was still floundering.

Could he help?

Maybe. He tossed around the negatives. Those pink fingernails made him wonder if there was too much city in Lake for her to stay away from the urban scene for long. Who knows—she might take her little brother and turn around any minute—hightail it back to "civilization"—as Cheryl had put it.

Nevertheless, she needed to brush-up on her outdoor smarts while she was here. He would help her with that.

As for himself, he'd never leave Shadow. How come the women he'd become involved with always ended up thinking he'd move to Denver or L.A. or something? They just didn't get it. Never happen. Nice place to visit and all that.

No, Montana was in his blood, he'd never leave.

Even with all his doubts, Hawk couldn't deny he was drawn to Lake. Her vision shone through her photographs. It fascinated him—as if she could pinpoint the heart and soul of a place.

Did she know her own heart as well?

And what about him? It's a whole lot easier to figure out someone else. Lake intrigued him, but what price would he pay if he took the dive?

He stared down the tunnel of the truck's headlights. Yeah, a guy could drown in Lake McDonald before he even realized he was going under. He grunted at his attempt at humor, causing Elle to rouse from her sleep on the seat beside him and give him a quizzical look.

Truth was, he couldn't seem to get his mind off her. Sure, she was nice to look at—but it was more than that—a certain beauty not defined by looks. A spirit, a talent... *and* a basket load of complications.

He wanted uncomplicated—didn't he? Simple was good. He was working toward simple. Simple had always been the goal... right?

The headlights flashed against the deep green wall of fir trees at the turn into the ranch. The truck took a hard bounce as it left the blacktop onto the gravel lane, prompting a sleeping dog to wake again and voice a serious, canine complaint.

NINE

Private Lessons

"What do you mean, don't get too tricky?" John Colter gruffed into the phone at his attorney. "Who's getting tricky? And what am I paying you for, to turn tail and run whenever there's a problem?"

"Well, no—just meant—"

"Don't just mean anything. I pay you good money to handle things for me, so handle it. Go find some photography expert to say those photos are real. I've given you plenty of resources—make certain you find the right experts." Colter added his own brand of emphasis to the word right. "I shouldn't have to tell you how to do your job. Whether you like it or not, I'm going with this, so make it happen . . . or I'll find someone who will."

Colter ended the call, disgusted. Used to be when he paid someone well to do a job, they'd get it done, no questions asked, not come sniveling back each time a minor detail got in the way.

Speaking of details, what was that meddling McDonald woman doing interfering in his business anyway? Her and that smart-aleck attitude she'd laid on him—and in front of everyone at the diner. Who did she think she was? Might as well pull her off her high-horse while he was bringing Matthews down. Matter of fact, the more he thought about it, he might be able to kill two birds with one stone.

He wouldn't admit it to the attorney, but it looked like he'd need a new and better plan than those photos. But, at least the photos of the dog would keep Matthews stirred up for a while. All the better, when he figured out what to hit him with next, Matthews would be looking the other way.

Yeah, he needed that gold mine. Needed it bad and he would get it. Those sure-thing, Asian stocks his hot-shot broker recommended almost bankrupted him. That mine could make him well. Gold was sky-high now.

"*Con-boy. Con-boy.*" Even now, at forty-one, the schoolyard taunt still echoed in his brain. He was in seventh grade, when his father was sent to prison . . . eight years for tax evasion. He and his mother had to scrape for every meal, every flea-bag apartment. She worked herself to an early grave, slaving at two part-time jobs which still left them hungry enough to eat the wallpaper. He was never going back to that.

Good thing old dad made useful connections in prison. When his father got out, everything was different; and he taught his boy to nurture those connections. Too bad everything was going down the toilet because of that stupid broker's hair-brained scheme. That's what you get for trying to go legit. He snorted. It was a private club John Colter had always been locked out of.

Well, they weren't going to win.

Lucky break, that old Barnes woman had shot her mouth off in the diner last fall, whining about her son, reminding him of the old Shadow mine. They had pulled plenty of gold out of that old mine, back in the day.

He had enough cash left to keep up the illusion that he was a mover and shaker . . . for the short term, anyway. These little towns were always looking for someone to infuse cash into the local economy. Couldn't keep up this pace for much longer though, had to get his hands on that gold mine. Pronto.

The Barnes woman was proving easy enough to play. All he had to do was pay the old broad a little attention, give her some sympathy, especially now that they had become such good "friends". Too bad so much of that mine was under Matthews's property—he was a different story.

If he was lucky, his photo idea could still work. Lake McDonald wasn't the only expert around. But his father had taught him, never count on luck. He needed action. Needed money. Needed that gold. He'd kill that condescending attitude of Matthews's, and in the process, strike a blow for his dead father. That testimony of Matthews's old grandfather had helped send his father to jail, left Matthews sitting up there on all that gold, acting like he's king of the world . . . like he didn't care about the gold. Who was he trying to kid? Everybody cares about gold.

Too bad his guy only knocked a glancing blow to Matthews's stupid mutt that morning on the road. That would have showed him . . . But he'd still have his chance. If Matthews wouldn't sell, he would take.

Yeah, John Colter knew the taste of misery. It was time Matthews got his plateful. No playin' around anymore. Maybe misery would knock him off that mountain. He'd work his other plan. This time, it would be fool-proof.

A plan that would open the way for him and leave Matthews's *begging* to get as far away from Shadow mountain as he could . . . for good.

***

Before Lake knew it, Wednesday rolled around and the little green Jeep was bumping its way up the drive to Hawk's place for her personal wilderness survival class. On the way, she'd almost chickened out and turned back. She'd even pulled wide onto the side of the road to make a U-turn, but the Scots-stubborn in her wouldn't allow it. When Hawk had called last night to confirm, Lake let him know that River would be in school, so he wouldn't be coming along.

Now, as she drove up to the house, she wished she did have River along for support . . . or perhaps, as a diversion. To Hawk's credit, he hadn't seemed to shy away from Riv. After Jeremy had turned tail and run at the mere mention of becoming her brother's guardian, it was a pleasant discovery.

Still, she mused, was this whole idea wise? How could a person dread and look forward to an encounter at the same time? Was it smart to even think about being near this man? He intrigued her, no getting around it. And, from a purely practical standpoint, she really *could* use the training. Needed it—if she were to continue her work in wilderness areas.

Rounding the last curve to Hawk's place, the tangle of thoughts was swept aside as she passed under the stylized, steel, "Shadowhawk Ranch" sign, supported by two large fir posts over the drive. A breathtaking panorama opened before her. The crisp, mountain air intoxicated her. Having experienced his ranch only once, during that mini-blizzard at the end of April—its current transformation, a mere month later was nothing short of phenomenal. The place was a living, breathing postcard.

The cabin stood in the middle of a clearing, which was now covered from end to end with velvety green carpet, spotted at intervals with sprinklings of various native flowers, predominantly yellows and whites, but with a few lavenders and blues sprinkled about. She'd need to learn the names. Gigantic Douglas fir surrounded the meadow. The shadowed areas within the groves looked dark as caves. Quite a contrast to the golden sunlight splashed across the meadow. Lake barely noticed driving the rest of the way up to the buildings, her attention so distracted by the scene downhill.

The jeep had hardly stopped rolling before Lake's instincts took over and she moved down into the meadow, camera in hand. Just a few quick shots. Good thing she had decided on the hiking boots instead of tennis shoes.

Oooo . . . One of the larger yellow patches of the as-yet nameless wildflowers near the edge of the meadow positively glowed from the light and drawing her like a bee to a flower. She readied the camera as she walked. Hmmm . . . for the best angles . . . a few shots approaching . . . interesting ones from straight above . . . another quick adjustment to the settings. Ignoring the damp grass, Lake was down on wet knees, crouched low to the ground, shooting upward from underneath the beauties with a gorgeous, blue Montana "big sky" as background.

"I could eat you."

A voice rumbled from close range and startled Lake enough to send her scrambling to her feet, barely catching her camera by its cord. At five-foot seven, she wasn't short, but Hawk loomed above her by a good half foot at least.

"That is if I were a hungry grizzly, and believe me, this time of spring, I would be very hungry."

A strong arm reached out and steadied her. Hawk's teeth flashed white against his tanned skin with a grin Lake thought might be as dangerous to a girl as a grizzly's.

"Hard to pass up a tasty morsel in my own backyard." Hawk tilted a look at her and finished with a quiet laugh, "You do get lost in the zone, don't you? We'd better get started on that lesson before you do too much more wandering, or the last picture they find on your camera might be of a grizzly's gaping mouth and a bunch of really big, sharp teeth." He laughed.

"Well, so long as I got the shot, I guess. It'd be a great one . . ." Lake said seriously, delaying her laughter long enough to let him wonder if she was kidding. When she released her laugh, Hawk's frown receded quickly and he joined her with a chuckle, shaking his head.

"I'm sorry I got distracted, it's so . . . I mean . . . this meadow is wonderful . . . I'm at a loss for words. I guess that's why I became a photographer." She shook her head, adding an apologetic smile. "It's a disease, I can't help myself. Sorry to keep you waiting."

"No problem. Glad you like it. My little piece of heaven on earth."

The smile Hawk wore went completely through him. Here was a man in his element, she thought, totally at home and comfortably at ease. She stood on the edge of the meadow locked in his smile for a moment, until she realized she was staring and an unexpected wave of shyness overtook her. She began examining the flowers at her feet. Hawk's gaze followed hers.

"Wild hyacinths." He said.

"Gorgeous blue." Lake answered.

"Yeah, I think blue might be my favorite color." He looked at her. "Used to be green, but lately . . . well, I'm finding I'm really partial to blue. Go figure." He mercifully released his hold on her gaze then and looked back at the flowers. "They'll bloom till late June, early July."

Flowers ... flowers ... Lake told herself. Talk about the flowers. "What are those little yellow ones at the edge of the woods?"

"Sagebrush Buttercup. They'll disappear here shortly."

"Pretty."

"Um-hmm. Just don't get the notion to chew on one of them. The natives used to crush up the petals and put them on meat to poison coyotes." He warned.

Lake's expression caused the corner of Hawk's mouth to twitch. Spurred on by her appropriate surprise continued, "They also crushed the whole plant and rubbed it on their arrow tips."

She backed up a bit from the deceptive beauties. "Huh—I had no idea."

"There's a treasure trove of medicinal plants and herbs out there too." He turned slightly and looked off down the slope. His hands rested on his hips. "Food too, if you know what you're doing. For instance, natives used to plan their spring migration around the flowering of the Bitterroot. They'd dig up the roots before they flowered and dry them. Too bitter to eat without boiling, though. They'd mix the boiled roots with berries or meat and make them into patties they took with them as they traveled."

"Oh, yes. I know that flower. The Bitterroot. Pink. Pretty. The state flower . . . I've seen them on Suzanne's menu."

Hawk's smile crinkled the tan skin around his honey eyes. "Well, we'll have to find some for you to look at in person. No menu can do them justice."

They both laughed.

"Speaking of treasure troves, you seem to have a wealth of information. Are you expert on all things Montana?"

He crossed his arms and considered. "I know my share. But the most important thing I know is, you can never know enough." His gaze rested on her face for a moment. "Like I said the other night, respect. That's the first lesson you have to get through your head. It's all beautiful. Awe-inspiring. Every day, I can't help feeling I'm one lucky son-of-a-gun to be here, but I never forget to keep my wits about me when I'm out hiking or whatever."

"I realize I have a lot to learn." Lake smiled. "I do tend to get into the zone pretty fast and tune out whatever else is going on around me."

"Yeah. I totally get that. Only I go into my zone in the safety of my studio." He motioned his head toward the larger of the two outbuildings on the property. "You, however, put yourself in a different situation out here." He made a broad gesture to the area. "We have to get you up to speed for your own safety. Lining up a reliable guide wouldn't be a bad idea, either. Have some eyeballs watching the woods while you're in your photog zone."

Another easy smile stretched across the lips Lake remembered all too well and she looked away toward the spot Hawk pointed to. Farther down the hillside, the terrain flattened out by a stand of firs.

"Those Wake-robins down there are pretty rare."

"Oooo, cool. What a cute name."

"Yeah, but, before you go crawling down there to take your pictures, you should know you might have some competition. Wake-robin roots are a favorite of bears."

Lake's mouth opened in a silent "Oh." at the info. "Thanks. I'll remember that." She narrowed a look at him. "How did you know I was thinking?"

"I also read minds, or didn't Sam mention that?"

Lake laughed. "No, I guess he forgot. Really—how?"

"Your eyes have been darting down there for the past two minutes. It wasn't hard to jump onto your train of thought."

"Am I that transparent?" Lake smiled.

Hawk's expression turned thoughtful. "In some things, but we've all got our walls. I think we've both smacked into a couple of each other's recently."

Lake thought about her walls. Yes, she did have them, one being a big bulwark constructed with Jeremy's help, matter of fact. Was the mortar too hard to withstand an invader, if he chose to advance? And just what kind of walls did Hawk Matthews have?

She kept her answer light, "Don't hurt yourself."

"I'm a big boy. I'll take my chances." His comment flustered her, but he grinned and nodded his head sideways toward the cabin. "C'mon, let's head up to the house. I laid out materials for today's lesson. We can do flora and fauna another day." He smiled.

So, he was thinking there would be another day?

"Okay. Let's go. I'm all ears."

"Hardly, but they are cute." Lake's stomach did a little somersault when Hawk tweaked the earlobe left uncovered by her braid.

They walked together to the cabin. Elle, who'd been observing silently, now did a "happy dance" around them as they walked, picking up a stick at one point and nudging Lake's leg. She obliged him and gave it a walloping throw. It landed halfway across the meadow.

"Niiiiice arm." Hawk exclaimed, genuine appreciation evident, as they watched Elle charge after it. He looked to her. "You didn't get *that* arm pressing a shutter. Impressive."

"Worthing Wildcats. Illinois State Softball runners-up, senior year. Center field. Thank you very much." Shoulders back, she lifted her chin proudly.

"Wildcat?!" The grin returned. "Oh yeah, that's good. I like that."

Upon reaching the door of the cabin, Hawk opened it with a "Ladies first. Or, should I say, Wildcats and dogs first?"

Elle pushed ahead of them, nearly knocking Lake off her feet. Hawk caught her shoulders and steadied her, until Lake's, "I'm good," made him drop his hands.

"Right . . . right."

It was Hawk who now appeared flustered. He diverted attention to the dog.

"Uh . . . You'll have to excuse her, she's used to being the lady of the house. And, now that it's out in the open that you're a wildCAT . . . well, can you blame her?" He winked. "But, really, she's just after her favorite spot." He nodded toward the big leather couch as Elle landed on it.

"Don't spoil her much, do you?" It was more comment than question. Lake already knew the answer.

"Ha. That obvious, huh? Well, let's just say we've been through an awful lot together. She's family. He hung his bark colored Stetson on the peg and ran fingers through his dark hair, attempting to push it back into place.

"Hat-hair. The bane of the cowboy's existence." He grinned, and Lake had to will her hand to stay at her side, squelching the notion to help him push a stray lock from his forehead.

"Here." He motioned to the dining room. "C'mon over to the table." The angled heels of his black boots thudded across the gleaming hardwood floors, adding exclamation points to every long, lean, levied stride.

"Let's start by covering some key items you should always carry with you when you're hiking."

He was being so hospitable, she was touched. She followed, taking in the "cabin" as they passed through the expansive living room with its tall windows, and rounded the massive two-way stone fireplace which anchored the center of the cabin, to the dining room. The place was great, glowing with golden woods and warmth, but the enigma in front of her held most of her attention.

He must be . . . what . . . early thirties? And the shoulders . . . And *holy-hunk* he was good looking. But no wife? No permanent woman in his life? Hmmm. What was the catch? He was knowledgeable. Lake knew he went to church, by Something Sam had mentioned. From the exchange in the meadow, she knew he had a sense of humor, which could be as, if not more attractive than good-looks. She sensed a spirit of fun that wasn't obvious at first. He could be charming.

Now there's a word a girl doesn't use often about guys these days. So, what was his deal? How come no girlfriend?

"Lake . . . Earth to Lake . . . Hey Wildcat." His voice broke through her thoughts.

"Oh, sorry . . . I . . . I was just thinking," she trailed off, too embarrassed to come up with a snappy reply.

"Yes, I could tell you were . . . thinking." He studied her, "I've been thinking a lot lately too."

Same wave-length?

Hawk pulled a chair out. She acknowledged the courtesy then, proceeded to be enlightened by his wilderness I.Q. The man's knowledge of outdoor safety was extensive.

He reiterated the importance of making others aware of your travel plans and expected return time. He explained the tendency of inexperienced hikers to get distracted and not follow those original plans.

"Being unfamiliar with the area, I'd advise you to take someone along as a guide—someone like myself, for instance," he added with a wink.

She was instructed on the use of a compass. Hawk was a big fan of carrying a GPS device, but still preferred to train his students as if they were not available. She learned about the search and rescue saying, "Cotton Kills"—a complete surprise to Lake—causing her to frown at her jeans.

"You can keep them on today."

He was having a little too much fun making her blush, she thought, but as he continued with his deadpan explanation and she wondered if the double entendre was all in her imagination.

"Cotton holds moisture to the body—lowers core temperature—whereas 100% non-natural fibers, or wool, don't. In this climate, hypothermia is a major killer. It's vital to keep your core—head, heart, lungs—warm."

He was all business.

"The main point I want to stress to you, Lake, is—don't get lost in the first place."

"Make it a rule to turn around and take a visual reference whenever there's a terrain change—so you'll be familiar with what the trail should look like going back. A crucial factor that a lot of beginners don't take into consideration. Nothing's going to look the same when you're traveling back the opposite direction."

He explained the need for mindfulness regarding the sun's position in the morning compared to the evening—

how it changes the appearance of the entire landscape, and how, upon coming to a divide in the trail, she should turn around and view it as if she were returning, in order to choose correctly. She then watched, fascinated, as he demonstrated how to make a highly visible night signal by tying a length of string to a chemical light stick and swinging it around in a circle.

"Here take these two rolls of flag tape, my compliments." He pushed the rolls of brightly colored tape toward her. "Every hundred yards or so, tie off a bit. If you don't have any, place three stones in a triangle to point in the direction you headed."

She learned, that she should carry a zip lock bag with a chlorine tablet and a piece of tinfoil to purify and collect water. How to stuff dry grass in your jacket to add insulation.

"There's always the old 'light the tortilla chip' for kindling." At Lake's gentle scoff, his dark brows knitted together, and he continued. It was as if he were playing the whole scenario out in his head.

"Although it's highly doubtful in that kind of situation you'd have tortilla chips handy. But it'd be great if you did."

"I'd probably be so stressed, I'd eat it."

He raised an eyebrow.

"Oh yeah. Stress? Bring on the chips. Big-time." She confessed.

"Well, try to hang onto one—just in case." He encouraged with a wink.

He was a warehouse of information, but where did the patience to teach come from?

"You've probably heard these questions a thousand times, from a thousand assorted greenhorns over the years. Why do you do it?"

She didn't know him all that well yet, but she could have sworn she saw one of his own "walls" go up just then. He rubbed a hand over his jaw line and looked out the window toward Shadow.

"Long story. Let's just say, if I ever do start to get impatient, I remind myself I could be helping someone to save their life . . . spare a family the pain of losing a loved one . . . someone from losing a friend." He turned back to her. "I guess that's what keeps me patient."

Lake knew a little of what had happened with him and his friend in the old mine when they were kids, but evidently Hawk didn't want to, or couldn't talk about it. Another wave of guilt washed over her about her initial judgment of him.

"Hawk . . ." Lake stood and turned toward the window for a moment trying to find the right words. "I hope you know, but I want to say this out loud. I've said it a hundred times in my head, but . . . I really owe you an apology . . . I mean, I admire your dedication . . ." She stopped for a big sigh. *Just say it Lake.* "You were right on the money when you said I needed to straighten things out with who I was really mad at . . . I needed to open my eyes . . . I mean . . ." Frustrating. The right words still weren't there.

Hawk came over to where she stood. "Listen." He tugged her braid. "Enough said on the subject. I did plenty of misjudging myself. Believe me, I am more than sorry about a lot of things."

"So . . . we're good?" Lake was relieved—or, wait—did he mean he was sorry about their kiss?

"I'd say we are. More than good." He gave another gentle tug to her braid. Lake was feeling she could become addicted to that smile of his.

Oh boy. She was falling fast. She didn't dare look up at him—he'd see too much. Quick. Diversion time. She reached for the mirror on the table and held it up.

"Take time for beauty?"

Her ploy worked.

"Ha. Right." Hawk took the mirror from her and walked over to a spot where the morning sun slanted a beam through the window. Catching a ray, he playfully bounced it at her face.

"Hey!" Lake blinked away from the light, wincing and smiling at the same time.

His deep laugh sounding through the room was like honey on warm, buttered toast. She was *so* hungry for that kind of laughter in her life again.

"Don't get your tail in a knot, *wildcat*. This," he maneuvered the mirror, and they both watched as the spot of light travel over the timber walls and ceiling, "can be your best friend if you're lost in the woods. Rescuers can see a light like this for twenty, thirty miles—easily. No object in nature does that. If you signal a likely spot—where searchers might see it, or a plane—well, you're halfway home."

"That's great, but how could you ever aim *that* at a plane?"

"Ahh, excellent question. I was waiting for you to ask that one. It's a bit tricky and takes practice. Come over here and look out the window, I'll show you."

Lake crossed over to the window and Hawk moved behind her.

"Okay, focus on an object. Pick a target. Let's see. Okay, see that spot about halfway up the slope?" He pointed to a large boulder in the distance.

She nodded, but wondered how in the world she was supposed to focus her attention on a boulder with this rock of a man so close. She could feel his body heat on her arms, and, she knew better . . . but couldn't resist inhaling that—man, plus mountain, plus magic of him. Whatever pheromones the guy was giving off put Lake right in the danger zone. What *survival* training was available for that?

Friends, Lake. Friends. She repeated to herself.

"That big boulder? We'll aim for that." He handed her the mirror. "Are you right eye or left eye dominant?"

This one she could answer from her photography experience.

"Right eye."

"Right, okay, right. So, hold the mirror up beside your right eye . . . Yeah, just like that. And hold your other arm straight out with your first two fingers in a V. Yes, there. Now, put that boulder right in the middle of that V."

Hawk brought Lake's arm up and helped her to get it into position. He bent to her level, their heads touching.

"That V is your sight. Now maneuver the mirror so the sunlight hits the boulder." His hand wrapped around hers.

It took a little bit to get the aim right, they wiggled her arm around a bit, but, all of a sudden, the spot of light landed on the side of the boulder.

"Ah. I did it. That is *so* cool." She spun in his arms with an excited smile, putting them just a heartbeat apart. His arms lingered.

"That's great, though you'll probably do it faster next time *without* my help." His eyes roamed her face. "I have to admit, I got a little distracted. Not like me." He gave an apologetic look. "I may have bumped your arm a little."

He was smiling slightly, but seemed preoccupied by another thought as his gaze ran over her hair, and landed on her braid. He picked it up and wound its length around his hand, lifting it closer to his face.

"Your hair . . . Umm. What is that by the way? Smells great."

Lids closed over the honey colored eyes as he inhaled appreciatively, trying to determine the scent.

Lake swallowed. She was having trouble finding her voice, distracted by the dark eyelashes while his eyes were shut—and then, by the little brown flecks that shown in the gold when he opened them. He was still holding her braid, lightly rubbing it between his fingers in a gesture causing Lake's knees to feel a bit weak. He smelled pretty amazing himself, though she wasn't going to say it.

"Um ... it's ... my shampoo, I guess. *Forest Meadow*, or something like that, I think." Out of nervousness, she blabbered on. "This has been very informative. You really know what you're doing."

The corners of his mouth twitched as the dark eyebrows raised and he searched her face. "I hope so. Time'll tell."

The exchange was making her a bit light-headed. His strength—mind, body and well—character, made Hawk a rock; and all at once, despite past experiences, despite swearing off men, she wanted more than anything, to take up rock climbing—right into those topaz eyes.

Hawk still held her braid, his hand rested against her cheek. Great hands. Capable hands. Warmth radiated onto her cheek as he tugged her braid, gently pulling her closer.

Hawk's head tilted slightly as he examined her eye color intently. "There should be a special name for that blue—really, unique." His mood turned serious. "Maybe—give it up-your lost blue—or drowning and I don't care blue?"

Warning bells. *Steady Lake.* She dragged her gaze from his eyes, but it just ended up landing on his mouth.

Was this foolhardy—or the best of common sense?

"Just relax. He knows what he's doing . . ." Hawk murmured, repeating Lake's earlier statement back to her.

The words brushed against her mouth just before his lips. It was like being home. She relaxed into the kiss.

Hawk released her braid, circled her in his arms and pulled her close.

***

So much for keeping his head about him, Hawk thought fleetingly as the feeling of Lake washed over him again. His senses spun. You'd think he'd never kissed a woman before. Whether this was the best idea of his life—or one that would sink him—not matter—he was in deep now.

He intended to impress her with his expertise today—but, not exactly *this* particular expertise.

About the time they both needed to come up for air, the mirror slipped from Lake's hand and clattered to the floor. She made a small sound of surprise. Whether from the clattering mirror or the kiss, he wasn't quite sure. They separated.

"Oh. I . . . I hope I don't' give us seven year's bad luck." Lake sputtered softly.

"Don't worry." He picked up the mirror, still intact, and returned it to her hand. "Unbreakable."

The mirror obviously—but as he studied Lake's face, he wondered—a hope emerged that he wouldn't have thought possible from their rocky start. Could whatever this was developing between them become unbreakable?

Her eyes gave a hint to the—caution versus hope—conflict that was waging in her, too. The gentle smile she blessed him with a couple of seconds later, seemed to indicate hope had won the day.

He stepped back with a parting caress to Lake's cheek. "Umm . . . Can't say I haven't thought about that, but I didn't plan on it happening today. Don't want to scare you back into a life of crime. A second, grand theft auto might not be so easy for Sam to ignore," he teased.

"Do I look scared?"

"No, matter of fact, you don't." He gave another playful tug to her braid. "A good sign."

Encouraged by her sparkle, Hawk found himself fighting hard against the urge to pull her back to him.

Lake caught a beam of sunlight with the mirror and playfully angled it toward an object on the mantle, using the V to sight it in, as he taught her. The sculpture's metal flashed a fiery, copper glint back at them.

"Good job. You have been paying attention." He smiled at his successful student.

"Oh, you've definitely gotten my attention." She followed her smile with a questioning glance from the sculpture on the mantle to Hawk and back again.

"One of yours?"

He walked over to the stylized bronze figure of a wolf, its head raised in a howl. "My first. I was fourteen. My grandfather thought the clay model I made was so good, that he took me to one of the foundries over by Bigfork and had it cast." He touched the bronze lightly. "He was my biggest fan, right from the start."

Hawk's eyes lingered on the piece, lost for a moment in a memory.

"This was your first?! Whoa. You're fortunate your grandfather recognized and nurtured your talent." Then more softly— "My folks did that for me too, I guess. We were lucky."

"Yeah, he saved me in many ways." Hawk ran his hand over the piece. "Helped light my path when things seemed pretty dark." He took a deep breath and exhaled slowly. "He's been gone eight years now. I sure miss the feisty ol' guy . . . His name was Aidan—my namesake."

A thought occurred to him and he looked up from the sculpture at her.

"Hey . . . I just realized something . . ." He said, grinning. "Aidan originates from an old Gaelic word for fire."

"Uh-oh." Lake frowned, quirking an eyebrow. "Fire and water? Doesn't sound like it bodes well for a relationship between us."

"Or—" He flashed an intentionally devilish smile her way. "Could make for a very steamy one."

Something went *thunk* in his chest when she laughed at his bold teasing. Oh—yeah—he could get addicted to that sound.

"It's good to hear you laugh." He squeezed her hand and tried cleared his throat so she wouldn't notice the catch in his breath that caught him off-guard.

He turned to the windows with an idea.

"It's a beautiful morning. Let's walk." He took her hand and led her toward the door.

TEN

Insights Outside

Hawk grabbed his Stetson from the peg beside the door and they stepped onto the porch, squinting into the late morning sun.

"Let's see. Which way for your first hike around the place?" He did a one-eighty. "This way." He pointed to a path leading into the trees. There's a nice trail that leads down along the stream. Shall we?"

"We shall. Looks lovely," she smiled.

"Hard to find a walk around here that's not." Was it just him, or were her smiles coming a lot easier—another good sign. He stopped momentarily to pat Elle, who, once she recognized which way they were going, bounded ahead like it was all her idea.

The path was wide enough for them to walk together and they set a quiet, leisurely pace down the gently sloping trail. Hawk spoke first.

"So . . ." He slanted a sideways look at her, considering. "*Lake McDonald.* It suites you. It *is* one of the most beautiful spots in Glacier Park. Let me guess—a favorite place of your parents?" His smile coaxed the same from Lake.

Their steps crunching on the rocky soil was the only sound for a few seconds before she responded. "Oh, you could definitely say that. You could say I kind of *got my start* there, if you know what I mean." She shot a sly glance at him, grinning. "And, with the last name McDonald, well, I guess my folks couldn't resist." Her grin faded as she looked at the sky and then their surroundings. "Nature photography was always their real passion—well, aside from each other," she said. He offered a hand to steady her over a rockier stretch of the trail, then she continued, "Glacier Park was about their favorite place on Earth."

"Here, come over here." He motioned for her to stand where there was a view through an opening in the trees. He pointed. "There. You can just see the tops of some of Glacier's peaks from here."

Lake's misty glance turned northeast, where, off in the distance, the majestic peaks of Glacier Park were just visible through the clearing.

Hawk smiled, understanding her feelings more than she knew. They walked on in silence for a distance. He thought to lighten the mood.

"Any other brothers or sisters—Brookes or Creeks wandering around?"

She smiled and shook her head. "Ha, ha. Nope. Just a Lake and a River."

He let out a low whistle that arched and dipped in amazement. "Whoa. How many years between you two?"

"Only twenty-two." She laughed softly. "Mom and Dad always wanted another child, but, had pretty much given up on the idea, when—*voila',*" Lake motioned with her hands, "twenty-two years later, here comes little bro." She produced a rueful smile. "I was out on my own by the time Riv entered the scene. I'd say we bonded pretty quickly after the accident, though . . . In a lot of ways, he's helped me through it."

"And you him. Must have been tough on the little guy. It's tough losing a parent anytime, but to be that age—" His frown remained.

Lake nodded.

"You're lucky to have each other . . . Makes you really question God at times . . ."

She frowned and shrugged her shoulders, his words hitting so close to home and her grief surfacing enough to halt conversation.

Hawk stopped beside some low boulders next to a crystal-clear stream. It gurgled merrily over rocks on its path down the hillside through the trees. You could have jumped it with a running start.

Lake dipped her hand into the cool waters. His sculptor's eye, fascinated by the graceful elegance of the line of her, watched in silence. Such a peaceful moment. Lake looked at home out here—or—was that just wishful thinking on his part?

She looked up at him then, and the emotion in those blue eyes almost knocked him over. He asked if she'd like to sit, motioning to a couple of boulders that were good sitting size. Although, he was probably the one who could use the sitting time more than Lake. She nodded and they sat quietly in the shady spot with their thoughts, appreciating the soft water sounds and occasional chirps and other mysterious noises from the tenants of the towering forest city around them

Lake spoke first. "When you said that, about questioning . . . you know, I'm still trying to figure that part out." She shook her head "I was really hurt—angry at God for a long time. I guess, deep inside, I knew it wasn't really helping anything, but I . . . it was so overwhelming . . . I couldn't make sense of it . . . Still can't really. Why me? And, for heaven's sake, why River? Why should he have to suffer like that?"

He reached over and smudged away a tear that had slipped down her cheek with his thumb.

"Our journeys." He pressed his lips together as he considered, looking off toward the mountains in the distance. "Yeah. Hard to figure—downright impossible—seems to me. But, we muddle along." He turned back to her. "I was where you are once, and I'm still trying to figure it all out . . . what I'm supposed to be learning along my way.

We'll have our answers someday, I guess. Till then, all we can do is pray—help each other..."

He stroked her cheek again, though no trace of tear remained and continued, "How's that passage go? Something about—how we now see through a glass, darkly—we only know part—but someday we'll be face to face with our maker and know the rest?" Hawk added a lopsided smile. "Excuse my paraphrasing."

***

Corinthians, she thought and watched his face. She too, recognized the power of the passage as it connected to her situation. And... how different it was to feel the strength of a man who was in touch with his strength—his faith. It, in turn, strengthened her. Heady stuff. Not something she had experienced with a man she was attracted to before. Now that she had, well, she'd never be satisfied with anything less.

They remained quiet for a couple of minutes, content to listen to the stream and the breeze, their senses taking in the peaceful scene. Through half-closed eyes, Lake stole a couple of glances at Hawk. She watched as he snapped off a long stem of grass and placed it between his teeth. He put his hands behind his head and settled back against the rock, eyes closed.

But, something Hawk had said earlier piqued her curiosity. She turned to him and, in a voice just above a whisper, "You said you have been where I am. Do you mind if I ask what you meant?"

He looked off toward the mountains, then removed the stem of grass he'd been nibbling at. He watched it as he spun it in his fingers, "I was nine when I came here to live with my grandfather. I was a Southern California kid. Mom and Dad and I lived there. They had a successful real estate business. Family business—Matthews's side." He shoved a little gravel around with the side of his boot. "When I was eight," he paused, "mom got cancer."

Lake winced.

"She fought," he sighed, "but, a little over a year later... She'd have had a chance now ... but, back then ..." He cleared his throat and Lake was sure her heart gave an extra thump. He stared at his boot and pushed more gravel around.

Hawk's chiseled profile was somber when he spoke. "Haven't talked about it much, just with my grandfather." A deep breath. "Anyway—after mom died, my dad kind of, well—fell apart. He managed to help it along though, by a lot of self-medicating—mostly booze." He paused momentarily, pushing more path gravel around with his boot. "I guess—while he still had some sense left, he sent me to up here to live with granddad—then drank himself into oblivion." Hawk snorted. "Record time—took him less than a year. My grandad tried to do an intervention, but..." He shook his head and turned back to her. "So—there you go. Not so young as River, but still—losing them both—"

"I'm so sorry."

Blue eyes locked with topaz. Her hand covered his without conscious thought. "You have been there. How did you ever—get over—it all?" She let the sentence trail off.

"Oh—yeah—I don't think you ever get over stuff like that. Cope. Have faith. Try to figure out what it is you're supposed to learn. My grandmother had been dead for about nine years when I got here." His hand turned over under Lake's and he held hers. One side of his mouth turned up as he looked to Lake. "Granddad had his own pain. First his wife, then his only daughter died . . . but he had a belief that pulled him through. Did his best to instill it in me. Saved me, I'm sure. I was a real mess when I showed up on his doorstep. Took him a few years, but between that and sculpting and all this," his hand swept out in a gesture encompassing meadow and mountain, "somehow I found a way to make it."

As he spoke, Lake could see in his eyes, that it was all still there, but he had evidently come to terms with it.

"When you think about it, nobody gets through this life without scars." He said softly. "Walking wounded. That's what we are a lot of the time." He picked up a little stone and sent it plopping out into the stream.

Lake was moved to add softly, "That's where faith comes in, I guess." She hesitated. "Or should . . . But it's so hard. I never expected to have mine tested in such a way. I kind of failed–" She picked up her own rock and tossed it into the water.

"Lake," he said gently, "Don't be so hard on yourself. Like I said, it's a journey—not a sprint. And there's a light at the end of the path. Just because you turn your head away doesn't mean the light has stopped shining. It's still there, to light your way, when you're ready. You'll get there."

He squeezed her hand.

Lake's stomach picked that opportune moment to growl. She blushed, adding an apologetic smile. "Oh. Nice. Embarrassing."

Hawk checked his watch and frowned. "Ah. You should have said something." He looked to her stomach as it growled again and laughed. "Oh, I guess you just did. I'm a poor host. How about, let's go back to the cabin and scrounge up some lunch?" He rose to his feet, grabbing Lake's hand and pulling her up.

"Oww." She cringed and couldn't help rubbing her backside a bit. Sitting on the rock had taken its toll.

Hawk grimaced and stretched a long leg. "We'll find more comfortable chairs, too."

"Don't be sorry. About anything. It's been good . . . getting to know you better, I mean." Lake said the last part quietly and turned her look sideways to check his reaction.

"Good. Then my 'make-up class' plan has worked." A satisfied smile spread across his tanned face, revealing those two dimples that fascinated Lake so.

They spent the next forty-five minutes enjoyably collaborating on, what they both agreed, were the absolute best BLT sandwiches either of them had ever eaten. But,

Lake was sure that, on her part, Hawk's company was the seasoning that made the sandwich so delicious.

While they'd constructed their sandwiches, it had given Lake an opportunity to watch him in his own environment. She'd clumsily tried to hide her interest, but was caught a couple of times. He just smiled. His eagerness to please was flattering. Considering the circumstances of their first meeting, She would never have pictured this cozy scene in a million years.

How things could change.

Hawk suggested fresh coffee to finish off their meal.

"I drink so much of the stuff, if I got a scrape, I'd bleed coffee," he kidded.

"I definitely drink my share," Lake said, "but I also make a mean cup of chai."

"Chai, huh? Never tried it."

"I'll mix up my special brew for you sometime."

"I'd willingly drink any potion you want me to." He winked.

It was becoming difficult to keep her heart thumping at a normal pace. "When do I see your studio?" she asked.

"Well," broad shoulders shrugged, "No time like the present. That is, if you have time today."

Lake looked at her watch. "I've got a couple hours until River gets home from school."

A whisper of doubt crossed her mind. "Oh, unless *you* are busy. When we were making lunch, you mentioned the

"Wilderness Wild" show coming up. I don't want to keep you from your work."

"Fortunately, my projects are almost wrapped up. I was stuck for a time, but lately I've been inspired." His smile was genuine. "I'd love to show you." He handed the GRRR emblazoned coffee cup to her. "Bring this. Spills are welcome in my studio."

She followed him out and watched as he slid the big, cedar barn door open, appreciating the muscles working under the blue chambray shirt.

"How large are these sculptures?" Lake asked, directing her attention to the oversize doors.

"Oh—uhh," he grunted as he pushed the massive door along it's track, then continued, "I did a twenty-one foot, copper grizzly for 'Wilderness Wild', for their headquarters down in Missoula. That's probably the tallest, so far."

Lake's jaw dropped. "How did you?"

"Two pieces. Then welded them together on site. There's a picture on the wall above the worktable."

She wandered over and looked at the photo of a group of people surrounding the impressive, stylized, copper grizzly, standing on its hind legs, paws flailing the air.

"Oh, wow. What a wonderful visual for their organization. Such power."

As she stared at the photo, Hawk came up to stand behind her, looking over her shoulder. She sobered at the sight of the beautiful blond in the picture, with her arm draped possessively around Hawk's waist.

Hawk followed her gaze. "The board members from Wilderness Wild. Great group. They're preserving a lot of land around here. Keeping the wild—*wild* for our children and their children and their children's children. I usually donate a piece for their yearly auction."

"Oh—a worthy cause. Generous of you. They . . . a . . .they look friendly," she tacked on the end.

With a raised eyebrow and a sideways glance, he realized her focus and continued, "Oh, yeah—the friendly woman to my right? Cheryl Winters. She was my agent."

"Was?"

"Yeah, well . . . I guess you could say she had a different idea where I was headed."

"Artistic differences?"

"Ha. That's rich." His frown morphed into a scowl. "Cheryl and I dated. She had big plans for me, or, I should say—us. Problem was, Denver was the center of her universe and all her plans revolved around me moving there." His laugh had a harsh edge to it. "Never happen. I'll never leave Shadow. Still feel kind of slow for not figuring her out sooner." He shook his head. "I mean, I'm not saying we didn't have some good times, and she landed me a few good commissions, but she figured I'd jump at the chance to get a big place in Denver and, how'd she put it? *–improve my situation.*" A splinter of sunlight glinted gold off his eyes when he turned his face toward her again. "She didn't know anything about who I really am."

Lake sat down on a stool and began petting Elle while listening to Hawk. The dog's tail wagged, stirring up a sawdust cloud from the concrete studio floor. She then proceeded to rest her head on Lake's thigh.

Hawk continued, "When things started to go south, she even let it slip that she didn't like my dog." He feigned a playful look of disbelief at the canine. "Can you believe it?" He squatted down and petted Elle, too. "No way. I can't believe it either girl." Then smiled at Lake adding, "You've heard the old saying, "*Love me, love my dog.*"

"I think I might've heard that one." Lake lingered in his look for a moment, then, losing her nerve, moved the subject away from the former girlfriend. "What's under the blanket?"

Hawk spent the next few minutes showing Lake the stainless-steel cougar and the smaller eagle he was crafting for the show. Impressed was an understatement. How could a woman ever think to try to remove this man from this place? It was obvious, he was in his element.

A sigh escaped her. "I envy you. You've found your place in the world." She traced her finger down the smooth silver line of the cougar.

Hawk watched Lake trail her hand down the steel of the cougar's front leg. He cleared his throat, "It's big country . . . I love it, that's true. Lately though . . . feels like something's kinda' missing."

"You're lucky you have Elle."

"You're right." he patted the dog again. "She's great." But he wasn't being put off. "What are you afraid of?" His voice held a husky note as he studied her.

She looked at him with a lopsided smile and raised eyebrow. "Let's see . . . apart from a terror of small planes—which you've already witnessed?" She smiled crookedly, then continued. "There seems to be quite a list forming. If you would have asked me a year ago, I would have honestly said—not much. But now, after the accident, with the responsibility of raising River, all my questions, and a year-long relationship over," she snapped her fingers, "just like that, I'm having doubts about my decision-making abilities."

Hawk's gaze narrowed. "Your decision about ending the relationship?"

"What? Oh. Jeremy? Oh—no. True colors and all that." Lake was past the initial hurt, now to the point she could smirk at the memory of his hasty retreat. "As soon as River entered the picture, it was—exit stage left." Another sigh. "It left me doubting my judgment—in men, for sure. I mean, why didn't I figure him out sooner?"

He searched her face. "One *man* is not *men*, Lake. Give the rest of mankind a chance." He frowned and tugged at her braid. "Let me rephrase—this man, anyway."

Then he opened-up that smile of his—broad and open as the big Montana sky.

She answered with her own. And it was more than the dimples. It felt good, *so* good, being in his company out here. Could Hawk Matthews be everything he seemed? She *wanted* to believe.

As Lake looked to Hawk, her eyes caught the time on the wall clock over his right shoulder. She would have to hurry to get home before River.

"Where did the time go? I've gotta run. Thanks again. For everything. Honestly. I had the best time here today, with you. Thanks." She placed a hand on his arm.

"My pleasure." He covered her hand with his. "First of many?"

She nodded and they walked in amicable conversation to her jeep.

They said their goodbyes and he didn't try to kiss her—which left her a little disappointed. But on the drive home, she thought more about it. Hawk knew she was at a vulnerable point in her life. If he didn't want to push her . . . well . . . he became all the more special for that.

ELEVEN

A Visitor

The next few days went by in such a flurry of activity that Lake had little time to daydream—probably a good thing. *Timeframes* was wrapping up ahead of schedule. There were frequent calls from her editor and quite a bit of correspondence to address from those using her stock photos. Business was picking up. Fran's son Tyler had really helped streamline her stock files over the winter. It was proving to be a big timesaver now.

River's excitement continued to build about Ranger Randy's upcoming visit to his school. Being the last week before summer vacation, he was bouncing off the walls, ready to be released onto the Montana wilderness.

Lake promised to take him on as many excursions as she could over the summer. He was all about that. Little bro was becoming a regular little tree hugger—and a pretty good artist to boot. She smiled and thumbed through his notebook. It was on his worktable, set up in one corner of the studio so he could work on his projects, while Lake worked on hers. River had an intense curiosity about everything outdoors. She had given him a notebook to keep track of his observations and he was diligent, in his six-year-old way.

Lake laughed to herself. Note taking definitely did not come from dad, but the love of the outdoors was all McDonald.

She set River's book down, picked up her Nikon and set out for her daily, pre-dawn walk, so grateful Fran was an early riser too. Not many sitters were willing to start their day at five a.m., and work a lot of split-shifts.

This morning, a surge of, what was it—confidence—self-assurance—peace? —about her decision to stay in Harmony came over her. Her long morning walks—taking her past everything from shopkeepers readying for the day, to the inspiring mountain views, filled with crisp air and the sounds of a world waking up—only herself and God—filled her up.

It was a kind of meditation.

She was steadily ridding herself of the discordant elements and doubts that had plagued her after the crash, feeling a new hope. *Harmony*, she mused. Yes, the music of life was blending together again.

She snapped an interesting cloud formation developing and spent a few extra minutes watching it, hoping the sun would catch the tops of the clouds with a bit more strength.

But, it wasn't to be this morning. She headed like a homing pigeon, from the park toward Suzanne's.

She checked her watch—just enough time to grab a quick cup of chai and a morning treat. Pecan roll or turnover? Decisions, decisions.

Lake was about to pull the door open to the café when it was pushed open from the inside by John Colter. He opened it for a sixty-ish, grey-haired woman. Dressed in blue-jeans and a flannel-shirt, she appeared wiry and fit.

The woman's gray-blue eyes examined Lake as she passed. Lake was pretty-sure she hadn't met her before. She smiled, and the woman smiled back, then turned to her companion. Lake avoided looking Colter. She hadn't run into him since she'd exposed his faked photos of Hawk's dog and she was concerned something inappropriate might pop out of her mouth—or his.

They passed and Lake entered the café. At the counter she stood, crooking her head slightly to watch them out the window.

"I know what you're thinking—odd-couple," said Suzanne, following her gaze from behind the counter.

"Oh. No. I wasn't . . . I mean I don't know . . . Who is that woman? She looked pretty hard at me, but I don't think I know her . . ."

"You meet her at Hawk's?"

Lake was taken aback by the fact Suz was aware that she'd been out to Hawk's place. Did Hawk say something? Oh, she had mentioned it to River. Must have been him.

Wow, news travels fast. The small-town grapevine was evidently alive and flourishing.

"Why would I see her there?" Lake frowned. "And how'd you know I was at Hawk's?"

"Ah." Suzanne reached over the counter and gave Lake's shoulder a nudge. "You two are perfect for each other. I can tell. I'm so excited. I said, from the first day you two were in here, there was a lot of electricity happening." She giggled and wiggled. "I'm so happy for you."

"Whooooa, slow down there, cookie. We're just . . . we're just . . . getting better acquainted. Don't start baking the cake yet." Lake shook her head, but it didn't seem to faze the grinning Suzanne.

"Oh. *Yes.*" Her hand went to Lake's shoulder again. "I can do that." Her eyes widened.

"Suzanne. Stop—really—full stop." Lake's cheeks pinked and she attempted to redirect the conversation, which had turned a few heads their way.

"Back to my question—who was that woman? Why would I have seen her at Hawk's?" Lake asked quietly.

"Monica Barnes? She's Hawk's neighbor. Forever. I thought you might have run into her there. Doesn't come in here too much anymore." Suzanne shook her head. "I don't quite get that duo, though."

They both looked out the window at the pair. Monica Barnes sat in the driver's seat of her blue Ford pickup with the window down, Colter still talking to her.

The name rang bells. Hadn't Hawk's friend Joey, the one killed in the old mine, been named Barnes?

"Is that the mother of Hawk's friend, Joey that—?"

"Yeah, the same. Sad story. No other kids. She's a widow. Never remarried. Can't see her being pals with the likes of Colter, though. Go figure."

Lake chose three cherry turnovers for River, Fran and herself, and walked down the sidewalk, casting a covert look in their direction, but, by that time, they were both driving away. Time for River to wake up. She didn't usually cut it this close.

"Mornin' buddy. Hey Riv, time to wake up." She said softly. "Big day today, remember? Ranger Randy?" She spoke in low tones so not to startle him awake. She hated being startled awake. It had happened enough to her over the last few months.

"Morning Lake!" River threw back the covers and hopped out of bed fully dressed.

Lake jumped about three feet.

"Ha, I fooled you!" He doubled over with laughter.

"Why, you sneaky little . . . possum." Lake tackled him on the bed and gave him a good dose of tickles. As soon as he begged her to stop, she did.

"What in the world? Did you sleep in your clothes last night?" Lake tried to frown at him. She'd been in to kiss him goodnight and tuck him in. The covers were pulled up tight around his chin. She angled a look at him.

River grinned sheepishly. "I wanted to be ready for today. I don't want to be late."

"River, you're never late."

"I know, but just in case. Hey, don't forget. You can come by the school and watch when Ranger Randy is there. Two o'clock. They said parents could come and I asked Miss James if it was okay if my sister came instead. And she said ab-sa-loot-ly. That means really, really okay."

Lake swallowed the lump in her throat at the thought of all the situations like this River would have to face. It could break your heart if you dwelt on it. She shoved the feeling away and continued with an extra dose of enthusiasm.

"I can hardly wait." She tickled him again and turned him toward the kitchen. "Now—breakfast. I bought a special treat for us this morning, cherry turnovers." He rushed to the kitchen at the mention of his favorite. "You can go as soon as you're finished."

Breakfast didn't take long. River was soon on his way to the corner to meet up with Zach for the walk to school. He was practically bouncing off the sidewalk. Lake watched him from the upstairs window till they met.

After River's repeated pleading, insisting, once again, that he wasn't a baby—she stopped walking him to school. But it hadn't stopped her from watching over him, or arranging with Zach's mom for the boys to meet and walk together.

She went down to the studio and rounded out most of the morning on the phone. Casey was fussing about a couple of details on the book. She'd called three times the past hour. When her phone buzzed again, Lake rolled her eyes and picked up.

"A strong cup of coffee. That's what you need." Lake told her.

"I'm always game for a strong cup of coffee. Can I consider that an invitation?"

Not Casey. Hawk's pleasant, deep tones—tinged with a chuckle resonated through the phone.

Lake brightened. He'd called on Monday to just to say hi, explaining he was tied up with a few finishing touches on one of the sculptures. The Wilderness Wild Show in Denver, was coming up fast. She hadn't talked to him since then, but he'd been on her mind all week.

"Oh, Hawk. Hi. I've been playing phone tag all morning with my editor. We're wrapping things up. She needs caffeine, though. Oh, and yes. Consider it an invitation." She checked her watch, at the same time doing a mental inventory of her fridge. "It's almost noon. I'll even throw in a couple turkey sandwiches with the coffee. Are you in town?"

Seeing him would give her just the jolt she needed, one that had nothing to do with caffeine.

"Just headed in. I'll be in town this afternoon giving a friend a hand, and then for class tonight. Got the crates for the Denver show packed this morning. Ready to hoist into the trailer. All that's left to do is celebrate. Turkey sandwiches with you sounds perfect."

Lake laughed. "I'm afraid my turkey sandwiches aren't really the stuff of celebrations."

"The *you* part is though. Slap those sandwiches together wildcat, and I'll see you in fifteen."

Thumpity-thump, thump. She could hear her heart. Game over. She was in deep.

She raced upstairs to the apartment and barely had time to scrape the sandwich fixings together when she heard the brass bell on the studio door downstairs tinkle.

He must be as anxious to see her as she was to see him. She grabbed for the dishtowel and swept at a few crumbs.

"I'm up here. C'mon up." Lake called.

Lake pulled a couple of her turquoise Fiesta Ware plates and coffee cups out of the cabinet. The coral napkins and placemats would accent nicely. She stood back and surveyed the colorful table as his footsteps reached the top of the steps.

Something was missing. Well, other than her shoes. She was extra glad she had given herself a pedicure the day before. The "Peek-a-Boo Pink" nails peeked cheerily at her. Back to the table. "Ah-ha." She spied the inexpensive bouquet of Shasta daisies—an impulse buy yesterday at the grocery store. She'd move them from the counter to the table. She was turning with the vase when the apartment door creaked fully open.

Lake couldn't have suppressed the smile on her face if she had wanted to, but she didn't want to anymore. All the bits and pieces she was finding out about Hawk . . . the challenges he had faced, his interests and passions and most of all the faith that guided him . . . she knew he would not hurt her. That confidence and security shone in her smile as she turned to greet him.

Her grandmother's cut-glass vase hit the tile floor and shattered into a thousand pieces. A complete stranger stood inside her apartment. A tall, menacing-looking, complete stranger. And being a small apartment, he wasn't all that far away. She took an involuntary step backward into the counter, wincing with pain as she stepped on a shard of jagged glass.

A grin hung loosely on the man's angular face, seemingly enjoying himself. Lake found her voice, while her right hand found its way to the heavy, Kool-Aid type water pitcher on the counter.

"Who are you? Why are you in my apartment?"

He laughed. "Why, you invited me in, Lake."

"I'm expecting someone."

"Oh . . . too bad." He glanced at the table. "Cozy." He narrowed his stare at Lake. "I'll get right to the point. *People* need to keep their nose and expertise out of business that doesn't concern them." Then ominously, "You know what I mean? . . . Do you? Do you understand what I mean," his hooded eyes raked her, "lovely Lake?" He finished with a crooked smile.

A smile that had nothing to do with happy.

Lake tried to keep her hand, and voice, from shaking, as she held the pitcher she would use as a club if needed.

"Oh, I know exactly what you mean. And I'll do whatever I feel like with my expertise. If *you* know what *I* mean." She stated defiantly. *What could be keeping Hawk?* She thought frantically. He should have been here by now.

The man's off-kilter smile disappeared at her defiance. He looked around the room. His leer landed on River's bright, smiling kindergarten picture, sitting on the entryway table.

"They're so cute at his age. So trusting." He turned back to Lake. "Know-what-I-mean?" He punctuated the veiled threat with a grin.

A grin that had nothing to do with liking children.

Lake was trembling now. Threatening her was one thing. She could to take care of herself, but the thought of someone hurting River was too much to bear.

"Get out. Get out now."

He stepped closer. Lake's grip tightened on the pitcher's handle, preparing to swing.

He ground out a laugh. A laugh that had nothing to do with humor.

"This conversation will be 'our little secret'. We know you'll make the *right* decision . . . for everyone concerned." His glance went back to River's picture.

He finished with a loud whisper, "Our secret." A dirty finger-nailed finger motioned a shhh over his narrow smirk. Then, he was out the door.

BEYOND THE SHADOW

Lake stood there, among the remains of the bloody daisies, as shattered as her grandmother's ornate, cut-glass vase.

***

Hawk hoped Lake liked the spur-of-the-moment bouquet of daisies he stopped to pick up, enough to justify his being fifteen minutes late. Two bunches. He smiled to himself and glanced at the flowers on the seat beside him as the silver truck pulled up to her studio. They were so like her, he thought. Those coral roses had caught his eye at first, with all their drama and scent, but the daisies possessed a simple beauty, an unaffected genuineness—like he sensed in Lake. He smiled at thought of her.

Lately, he'd been doing a lot of smiling.

The studio was empty, but he could see the door to her apartment was ajar. He took the steps two at a time.

"Knock, knock . . . Sorry I'm late but I . . ."

It had been a long time since Hawk Matthews's jaw dropped open in surprise. Make that alarm.

Lake stood there, in a pool of blood and daisies, holding a pitcher.

"What? What *happened*? Lake . . . *Lake*!" Then as the bare feet and broken glass registered, "Don't move. I'll come to you."

She was white-as-a-sheet and wide-eyed, and it sent a shock to the core of him like he'd never experienced before. Even after all he'd seen working with GRRR, the sight of Lake's blood hammered him as hard as anything he'd been exposed to. Had she had another PTSD episode? Not good. He tossed his own daisies onto the table, took the pitcher from her and put it on the counter then carefully lifted her out of the bloody, shattered mess. He took her to one of the kitchen chairs and propped her bleeding foot on another.

"Keep your foot up. I'll be right back."

Rifling through the kitchen drawers produced a couple of flour-sack dish-towels. After placing her foot on the towel, Hawk gave it a quick examination. The cut by her left heel was deep and still bleeding quite a bit.

"Looks clean, but, I can't tell for sure. A doctor should look at it. You'll need a stitch or two. The way it's bleeding—looks like you might have nicked a vein."

Lake snapped back to reality.

"Oh . . . no. It's just a cut." She frowned deeply. "Are you sure? I h-have to clean up this mess. I need to go to River's school this afternoon. I need to be there at two. Absolutely have to. Ranger Randy is going to be there and I promised River. I promised."

Her eyes teared. He looked at his watch. "It's ten-to-one. Let's get you to the clinic and see if we can make it. No. Don't try to walk. I'll carry you. I'll take care of that," he frowned at the bloody floor, "later."

"But . . ."

"No buts. Try to relax. It'll be all right. Really."

Silken strands of her hair had loosened and he gently pushed them from her face. He lifted the dark braid over her shoulder and rubbed her back a little. His soothing didn't seem to be having much effect on the state she was in. He wrapped the towel tighter around her foot and carried her to the truck.

All Hawk could get out of her on the way to the clinic was that she dropped the vase and cut her foot. That she was clumsy . . . It had been her grandmother's and she was disappointed. He gave her a sideways glance. She was staring out the window. Why was she avoiding looking at him?

Something didn't add up. What was the deal with the pitcher? What was she doing with that? Why would she pick up a pitcher when she was standing barefoot in broken glass? No—he knew he wasn't mistaken—knew what scared looked like. Had seen it on countless GRRR rescues. Acknowledged it in himself when he needed to.

And Lake was scared. Very scared.

Was it the sight of the blood? He hadn't pictured her as squeamish—but there was a lot of blood.

Whatever it was, he wanted badly to help her. If the PTSD was worse than she thought, well, he would help her deal with it. It was important to him for her to be whole and happy. Matter of fact, he had to admit it to himself, Lake's happiness and well-being was fast becoming his number one priority.

Just when exactly, had that happened? It was his turn to stare out the window.

Hawk helped her to the exam room then went to the waiting room and walked it like a caged animal, causing an older gent to ask him if 'it was his first?' He frowned, then understanding, shook his head, not bothering to explain further. Hawk knew her injuries weren't serious, but he wished she'd open-up to him. Trust him to understand. If they couldn't develop trust... Well...

He brushed his hand absently through his hair and plopped down into a chair, leaned his head against the wall behind him and closed his eyes. Tried to quiet his thoughts. *Here I am again. Asking for more favors... Please... Let her know she can trust me...*

***

"There was a small piece of glass lodged in the wound. The X-ray showed it clearly. Tricky." The doctor smiled in satisfaction as held up tweezers with the glass shard to the light. "Good thing you came in. The cut is more on the side of your heel. You should be able to walk normally on it in two or three days. Until then, try to step lightly. Keep your weight on the toes on that foot. Keep it bandaged and dry. Favor it for, um, let's say, three days and come back if it turns red or hurts more than it does now. The stitches should dissolve by themselves."

"Thank you, Doctor." The nurse helped Lake to the wheelchair and rolled her to the waiting area. Lake used the time trying to decide what to tell Hawk.

She had a mind at war with itself, wanting, in the worst way, to tell him about that goon's threats. But the threat to River was not to be taken lightly. She couldn't afford to make a mistake. What was her best course of action?

When the nurse wheeled her around the corner into the waiting room, Hawk immediately came to her side. He took over wheeling her out to the parking area. Once there, he put his arm around her waist, to take the weight off her injured foot while he boosted her into the truck.

"I can't thank you enough for helping me out. Some celebration." Her mouth turned down.

"No need to thank me. We'll postpone celebrating. I want a raincheck on those turkey sandwiches."

The man could make her smile. "You got it."

He shook his head. "I would've been there sooner, but I made a side trip," he said frowning. "If he hadn't stopped for the flowers, this whole scenario might not have played out this way. Unlucky break."

"Oh. Yes. I saw the daisies. They're lovely. Thank you. I hope they'll be okay till we get back." In the warmth of his gaze, she blushed. "How did you know they're my favorite?"

"They said *Lake* to me," he said, bestowing one of those easy, open smiles of his on her.

Lake wondered, how did he do that—make everything in the world seem okay when he smiled? Her gaze lingered for a moment, until another smile, a stranger's sinister one from earlier in the afternoon popped back into her mind. She blinked and looked away, reality crashing in on her again.

What should she do? Tell him? Would it put River more at risk? She prayed for guidance. Inwardly, she was still panicking and found herself greedy to stay in his presence—soak in as much of strength and warmth as she could.

It was then the realization flooded over Lake, that some prayers are answered quickly.

A feeling of trust swept through her.

She would tell him everything—right after the program at River's school. They drove straight there. It was two o'clock, on the dot, when they slipped into the back of the classroom. The show was about to start. It was crowded, but Hawk rounded up a chair for her. River had obviously been watching for her and beamed when he spotted them, waving a little wave. One for Hawk, too, she noticed.

The exchange further cemented her decision to tell Hawk everything.

She was surprised her attention could be diverted from the past couple hour's events, but the show was a lot of fun to watch. Hawk left to help with the animals. "Ranger Randy" was the friend Hawk was coming to town to help that afternoon. Randy Stewart was another GRRR team member. His "Ranger Randy" was a part time gig.

Lake watched as a parade of Montana creatures passed by the students. All the animals were rescues and unable to return to the wild.

There was the one-winged eagle, still majestic, whose existence had been forever changed by a sadistic shooter who was never caught. Ranger Randy explained that he had constructed a high perch on the reserve, out of a downed Douglas fir, that the eagle could kind of hop up and down like a spiral ladder, satisfying, in some part, its desire to scan great distances.

The big timber wolf had been rescued from private ownership. It was found years ago, starving, with a log chain around its neck. Now, it had peace on Randy's little reserve, just outside of Harmony. The wolf was old, but still beautiful.

There were smaller animals too, like marmots and ground squirrels and such. River was transfixed. More than once, Hawk caught her eye and gave her a wink—both enjoying River's enjoyment.

The hour flew and soon it was time to leave. River had another half-hour of school. Hawk helped Lake back to the truck. She checked his watch. She could have looked at the dashboard digital, but it was nicer to look at him.

"I'll have to hurry to get that mess cleaned up." She frowned.

She told Hawk she absolutely needed to pick River up from school today. He gave her a quizzical look, seeing as how the school was only a half-mile away, but he said he'd pick River up after he got her situated.

Then, tipping a look at her which broached no argument, "And like I told you, I'll do the cleanup."

She conceded with a relieved smile. "Okay. I'll take you up on both."

Lake noted Hawk was extremely somber when he came away from the clean-up task. There had been a ridiculous amount of blood for such a little cut. Good thing River didn't see it. She explored his expression. Surely Hawk must be hardened to the sight of blood, especially being on the GRRR team and all.

He stood near the door and looked at her, searching her face.

Lake broke the silence, "You better go get River, but after he's home, there's something important I need to talk to you about. We'll need to talk in the studio, though, away from River."

Still silence, but her statement seemed to trigger a decision in him. He walked over to her and picked her gently up out of the chair, taking her weight against him, off her injured foot. His right hand cradled her head.

The hungry kiss that followed this maneuver was something that hadn't been on Lake's map. She wasn't even aware this place existed. If she had, she would have been searching for it in earnest. Warm waves of emotion washed through her as they explored this new vista together. More than physical, it tasted of acceptance, trust, and placed a whole new horizon in front of her.

They parted breathless. She'd never seen Hawk smile, so wide. After a long look, he gave her a firm but too brief hug, and planted a kiss on her. This one, accompanied by a growl and placed smack dab in the middle of her forehead. He sat her back down in the chair.

"Hold that thought." He winked. "We'll pick up this discussion when I get back."

**

As Hawk swung himself into the big truck to pick up River he was still feeling a surge of relief, well, among other things, he grinned. He knew Lake had turned a corner and made the decision to trust him. Trust. And that was a powerful thing.

Thank You, he thought.

TWELVE

A Hawk Grounded

"Lake! Lake! . . . Lake! Where are you?" River charged into the studio snagging the brass bell hanging on the door with his backpack strap, sending it on a ringing roll across the spruce floor.

Lake jumped up from behind her computer, wincing as she forgot and put weight on her heel. "I'm right here Riv. Slow down. Whoa . . . Whooooa. What's the matter?" She hurried to intercept him, concerned. "What is it? You okay?" At his affirmative nod, she continued, "Where's Hawk?" She crooked her head, searching out the window, hands on River's shoulders.

"That's what I'm trying to tell you! Hawk had to go. We were almost here and his phone rang . . . Only it rang like a dog growling and barking Lake. That's how his phone rings. It was FUN—NY." He saw her bandaged foot. "Hey, what happened to your foot?"

"I dropped a vase of flowers and stepped on the broken glass. It's just a little cut, Riv. It will be okay, don't worry about it." Lake smiled at him and tried again. "Where is Hawk?"

His little brows knotted into a frown. "He said . . . umm . . . He said to tell you he'd call you."

"What? Why didn't he come in?" She hopped over to the window, foot throbbing. This didn't make sense.

"That's what I was trying to tell you! He had to go rescue somebody!" He could barely contain his excitement. "He's gonna go help find some people. Up in the mountains." He ran to the stairs. "I'm gonna go upstairs and turn on the TV. Maybe they'll say something 'bout him. I'm gonna call Zach." He raced up the stairs to the apartment.

"What did—" But she could hear that River was already in front of the TV.

Lake made it up the steps at a pretty good clip by holding on to the railing and hopping on her right foot, only using her left toes for a little balance. Her foot continued in throbbing mode, but that's not what occupied her mind. She and River searched the local channels for news. After a couple of minutes–bingo. A breaking news logo flashed across the screen, followed by a local reporter.

***

"State Senator Loren Calhoun, actor Bradley Thompson and two others, returning from a fishing trip in Northwestern Montana are reportedly missing at this hour. Shortly after three this afternoon, the chartered float plane's

BEYOND THE SHADOW

pilot reported to the Kalispell airport the plane was experiencing engine trouble moments before radio contact was lost. The plane was believed to be somewhere over the northeast quadrant of the Bob Marshall Wilderness Area. Shown here is a live clip of area search teams mobilizing across the region to search for the missing aircraft. Stay tuned to Action News Nine for breaking updates and a full story at six."

***

The live clip they showed was of the Glacier Rescue Rapid Response team getting ready. Sure enough, there was Hawk and two other men in orange jumpsuits—GRRR logos emblazoned across their backs, standing next to . . . a plane . . . Oh, dear God, no . . . Her stomach lurched. The aircraft was identical to the one their parents crashed in.

She looked to River. Unfortunately, his memories of the plane their parents went down in were still vivid. The news stations must have shown that clip of them getting in the plane that day, a hundred times. Lake had to carefully monitor River's viewing for quite a while, and still missed one occasionally. The GRRR plane was a match, down to the color.

River went silent. The station returned to regular programming. Still nothing from River. He continued staring straight ahead.

"I'm sure they'll be okay Riv." She put her hand gently on his head.

River looked up at her. "That plane . . . it looked like the one . . ."

"But it's not the same one, Riv. We can't think about that. Besides, Hawk told me he goes up in the helicopter, not the plane. Didn't you see the helicopter in the background? That's what Hawk would be going up in—if they use it at all. A lot of the time, they take trucks, or motorcycles, or hike in sometimes. They've practiced a lot, Riv. Experts check all their equipment."

Was she trying to convince River—or herself?

"They'll find those people and help them out. I'm sure Hawk will tell you all about it when he gets back."

"Should we say a prayer for them?" He was searching for a way to help. Her eyes got watery at.

"That's a great idea. I think it's the very best thing we could do for them right now." She kissed him the top of his head. "You know what? You're one, smart kid."

River led their prayer in the sweet, clear voice of a believing child, "Please help Hawk find those people and please help them not to get hurt. Especially Hawk. I don't know why you wanted mom and dad to be with you more than with me, but I really hope Hawk can stay around for longer. Oh, and please help Lake's foot be okay. Oh, and thank you for all the animals at school today. And please help the animals from being hurt. And thank you for summer vacation. Amen."

Lake hugged River tightly. It gave her a few more seconds to try and swallow the huge lump in her throat and blink back the tears. "Amen."

Bring the little ones to me. A question glimmered through Lake's head—aren't we all *little ones*?

The prayer seemed to help River a lot—Lake, not so much. Her mind skipped back to frantic prayers she said for their parents. Why couldn't she stop the thoughts? Disappointing. Still so near the surface . . . Would it ever be different? She didn't know, so she prayed about that too.

But mostly, she prayed Hawk would be safe.

In the middle of one of those prayers, Frank Effron, the older man who had been nervous about teaching last week's class, called to let Lake know he would be teaching tonight. There was no way Lake could imagine going now. She couldn't focus on anything except Hawk and any news. She thanked Frank for calling, but used the cut on her heel as an excuse.

She and River ate a quiet supper, talking a little about the animals that Ranger Randy had shown them that afternoon. Thankfully, between that and attempting to draw the animals they had seen kept him occupied for most of the rest of the evening.

The six o'clock news hadn't offered much more than the bulletin. They kept repeating the same information over and over, wording it a little differently. They went into detail about Senator Calhoun, who evidently was quite a celebrity around here. Played pro football in Denver for a while, back in the day. Naturally, they spent a profuse amount of time reporting on Bradley Thompson. At thirty-two, the actor already had two Oscar nominations under his belt and the entertainment world constantly discussed the actor.

Lake had met Thompson once on a shoot. A brief meeting, but he had been surprisingly down to earth. She prayed for him, too.

River was off to bed at eight-thirty. Tomorrow was the last day of school and he was ready for summer vacation. Lake turned the TV on, but hit the mute button, glancing over every so often for new developments. So far—nothing.

After putting a meatloaf together for tomorrow and busying herself in the kitchen for a time, she pulled a couple of recipe books out and absently flipped through pages. Nothing sounded good.

Lake reached over and touched the soft petals of the daisies Hawk brought earlier. He had used her make-shift water-pitcher weapon for a vase. So cheery. She stared at them, pictures of Hawk flashing through her mind as if she had taken them with her camera. That's just how her brain was wired.

Sometimes a blessing, sometimes a curse.

Lake glanced up at the clock for what must have been the fiftieth time. Eleven thirty-seven. *Uh . . . Torture.* Was he in the air right now? Searching in the dark? She hoped not.

That's what he does, Lake.

Was she strong enough to cope with this on a regular basis? Was it smart for her? For River? Her little brother was already becoming attached to Hawk after only a few meetings. Probably only natural for the little guy to look for a strong male role model now that dad wasn't here . . .

All her fears about having a relationship with Hawk, washed over her in a huge, capsizing wave. She'd been floating her boat on denial, she grimaced, and she couldn't pretend any longer.

This was the reality she had been pushing to the back of her mind. Hawk the sculptor—she could easily relate to. They shared an artistic temperament and world view that, though they practiced their art in different fields, was, in reality, quite similar. That was a Hawk she could soar with.

But the GRRR Hawk . . . that was also a huge part of who he was—*is*—she flinched. They were both part and parcel of the same man. Was she kidding herself? Lake picked up her phone from the counter and hopped her way over to the couch. She lay down and curled up in a tormented knot, phone in one hand, remote in the other, the flickering flashes from the TV's nonsense the only light in the room. Was she strong enough to deal with this kind of mental torture? Should she put an end to this before it went too far?

If only her faith was stronger. Another thing they shared, but Hawk's was so much steadier than hers. But, if she truly believed . . . Lake wanted Hawk in her future. Could she deal with the fear? Let her trust . . . and hope again? Or let fear rule. As she laid there drowsy, but unable to sleep, a simple bit of verse from somewhere. It came out of nowhere and slipped into her head, about *"casting all your worries on Him, because He cares for you"*. Her mind grasped at the lifesaver she'd been tossed and she dozed off.

Casting . . .

***

Billowing, dark, grey, storm clouds were flying past the studio windows at a *Dorothy in the tornado* rate . . . Her phone was ringing . . . Or was it a dog barking? How did her phone end up in the middle of the room . . . on the floor . . .? She had to get it . . . It might be Hawk . . . She tried to get up, but . . . Oh. Both her feet were wrapped together with the hospital gauze . . . She fell.

"Uhh."

Disoriented, Lake sat up on the floor beside the couch, the coverlet tangled around her feet. She rubbed her face.

What?

A dream. She frowned, trying to make sense. Her phone *was* ringing. Lake tried to focus, reaching frantically for it, knocking it off the coffee table and crawling after it on the floor, fumbling to answer. *Hawk*. She flung it open.

"Hawk, I was so . . . Hawk?"

"Lake. No. It's me, Sam."

"Sam? What? Oh." She sank back to the floor. "No. Please, no."

"No. No, Lake. No—nothing like that. Hawk's alive. Not exactly okay, but he's managing."

A qualified relief washed over Lake.

"What happened? Is he hurt? How is he? Where is he? He hasn't called . . ." She fired out the questions faster than Sam had any hope of answering.

"Slow down, Lake. Sorry I couldn't give you any news sooner, but they had to fish him out of the crash site."

Lake's eyes widened in alarm at "fished out".

Sam continued, "It was a bit tricky. Deep in the trees. Really a miracle no one was killed. They got everyone out. GRRR got to them first. Broken bones, concussions, but they'll all make it. Textbook rescue . . . that is . . . up until it wasn't."

"What do you mean? What happened to Hawk?"

"He was the last one being hoisted back up to the chopper, when, I still can't believe this, but a fastener on one of the cables snapped."

Lake's stomach turned.

"How bad? Tell me the truth." Her knees went weak . . . her stomach went to her throat.

"Relax. He's tough . . . and trained. Luckily, if you can call any of it lucky, he was only about eight feet off the ground when it snapped. Hit the ground hard. Doesn't think anything's broken, but, the worst of it was the steel cable fastener cut his thigh when it snapped."

"Is he okay now? Is he at the hospital?"

"He's at the hospital in Kalispell. They're working on the leg now. He lost a quite a bit of blood. Needed a transfusion."

A blood transfusion? Lake struggled to her feet . . . make that her foot. "I'm coming down. As soon as I can find someone to stay with River. Call me if you hear anything more, please?"

"Sure thing."

"And Sam—"

"Yeah?"

"Thanks. Thanks so much for calling me."

"Sure. I know he'd have wanted me to."

***

Lake managed a quiet kind of tiptoe on her injured foot into River's room after calling Fran. She sat on River's bedside and softly explained what Sam had told her. She told him that Hawk had cut his leg and was in the hospital. That she wanted to go see him.

"So, when you wake up, Fran might be here to help you get ready for school."

"God heard us." Riv said sleepily.

Lake gave him a little hug and kiss. "He always hears, Riv."

Lake re-tucked his covers and did her modified tiptoe out of his room. She hopped down the steps after that and met Fran at the studio door.

Fran was amazing. She was there in ten minutes.

"Hi hon." Fran gave her a big hug. She noticed Lake's foot. "How are *you* doing?"

"Oh, I cut my foot on some broken glass. Long story. But, if I'm not back in time to get Riv off in the morning, would you please drive him to school tomorrow? It's important. I don't have time to explain now, but it's a safety issue. You'll probably have to pick up his friend Zach too. His mom's number is on a list by the phone. And please make sure they get into the school before you drive off. I'll explain later."

Fran shook her head yes, with a frown.

"Good, but, right now, I want to get to the hospital."

"Of course, you do. Don't worry about a thing here. Go. Go." She pushed at Lake to go out the door.

***

Thirty-five minutes later, Lake hobbled through the automatic doors of the hospital in Kalispell, to the whoosh of antiseptic smell and whirlwind of medical and rescue personnel trying to make their way around the media throng. Efforts were currently under way to herd the crowd into a large conference room. Looked like the staff was having a time keeping them corralled, though.

Their vehicles, complete with satellite dishes and antennas, lined both sides of the road leading to the hospital and took up most of the parking lot, which had forced Lake into a parking space at the edge of the solar system.

Her foot was throbbing again, although her own injury didn't concern her right now. Hawk's did.

The information desk was hopelessly crowded, so Lake opted for a nurse's station, and was promptly sent back to the information desk, where, after waiting for almost half-an-hour, they wouldn't give her any information anyway.

She wasn't family.

Tired, aching and frustrated, she spotted an open chair. A rare commodity. Regroup and form another plan. She'd pictured herself just walking in and finding out how Hawk was doing... Maybe even getting to see him...

Bleary eyes searched for a wall clock. 3:06 a.m. Yikes. This had been one monster of a day. How long could adrenaline keep you going? She slumped forward, elbows on knees, head in hands.

The uniformed legs of a group of law enforcement types walked rapidly by, one pair skidded to a stop.

"Lake? What are you doin' there?"

She looked up. "Sam—they won't tell me anything. I'm not family." She stated flatly.

He shook his head, and scanned around. "This place is crawling with reporters." He glanced at her bandaged foot. "Looks like you had some tough luck yourself."

"Broken glass. It's nothing." She waved the mention of her injury away.

"Stay here. I'll be right back."

Sam walked over and spoke quietly to his group, causing heads to turn in her direction. After several nods, they proceeded down the hall and Sam came back to her.

"Come with me Lake." Sam stopped by the nurse's station and hijacked a wheelchair, rolling it over and pointing for Lake to get in.

"Oh, Sam... I don't..."

"Please don't argue. It'll save you some hurting and me some time. Hop in."

Sam was right. He negotiated the corridors in no time. They pulled to a stop in front of a recovery room and he spoke to the nurse standing outside the door who was examining a chart.

Sam was back in a moment.

"Lake, listen, I got the okay for you to go inside for a few minutes."

His brows compressed in a look of concern.

"I want you to be prepared. He's pretty bruised up and has lots of stuff hooked up to him right now. Mostly precautionary. He took a hard fall—bruised ribs and his face is beat up. Well, he's basically one, big bruise. The most serious injury was the cut in his thigh." He shook his head. "Thank God his helmet kept him from being knocked unconscious from the fall. He stopped himself from bleeding out. Missoula Rescue's chopper was only a couple minutes away. They fished him out." He finished with a wry smile, looking toward the room. "He's excited about that." He gave a short laugh. "There's quite a rivalry between the two groups."

She didn't know a whole lot about first aid, but she did know the femoral artery went down through the thigh and a cut to that could be fatal. Quickly. She was thankful she was still sitting.

"Oh." She swallowed hard, but couldn't say anything more.

He stood and rubbed her shoulder. His smile reappeared.

"Hey. Not to worry. He's supposed to keep still. He's pretty drugged up and has been fading in and out. So, take it easy on him." He smiled a sideways smile, teasing, "He seems to lose his cool around you."

Her tension eased. If Sam was laughing, things couldn't be too bad.

Lake tilted her head at him and smiled back. "I promise, I'll be on my best behavior. Thanks again." She stood and gave him a hug.

"I've got a few things to sort out here; then I need to pick up Slug and Elle. They're over in the office. I'll take Elle to my place for the time being. After that, I'm gonna hit the sack for a few hours. You should too. I've got a mountain of paperwork ahead of me tomorrow." He grimaced. "But it'll feel pretty good, considering everyone made it out of that mess alive. I'll probably see you tomorrow. Night."

With a parting squeeze to Sam's hand, she steadied herself, and peering around the door, stepped in, Sam's warning at the forefront of her mind as she did. Even though she knew Hawk was going to be all right, she still weakened at the sight of him lying in the hospital bed.

The recovery room was well lit for three-thirty in the morning. There was a curtain three-quarters of the way around his bed. He was hooked up to several monitors blinking messages and bottles dripping liquids.

What she saw at his bedside made her almost light-headed. One side of Hawk's face was scraped and swollen, the skin reddened now, but she was willing to bet it would be purple by morning. Same with his left arm, from what she could see.

He was out of it. Sam said he might be. She quietly moved a chair to his bedside and sat, blinking back tears. His right hand didn't look too injured, so she reached out and took it with both of hers, kissed it and laid her cheek upon it.

"Lake . . . here." The rough whisper was groggy, but oh, so good to hear.

She raised her head to see the warm eyes open a slit.

"Hawk. I'm here." She couldn't say anything more. All she could do was look into his eyes and give his hand another soft kiss.

He groaned. "Uhh . . . kiss it . . . make it . . . bett . . . er." He even managed a little dimple, before a frown creased his brow. "Shhorry . . . gave me shhome shhtrong shhh . . . tuf." Another frown. "I dunno . . ."

"Don't try to talk. You need to rest. I should let you sleep. I'll come back in the morning, after you've slept. I'm just so relieved you're going to be okay. I don't know what I would have done . . ." she told him softly, from the heart.

His eyes were already closed when he mumbled, "Mmm-nnight . . . love you . . ."

Then he was out of it again.

Lake blinked—straightened—then stared. his eyes were closed—hers were opened.

She sat there for a few more minutes, her thumb rubbing the back of the capable hand. The strongest man she'd ever known, now completely relying on other's strengths. She searched his face. The "shhome shhtrong" stuff they gave him must have really sent him for a loop.

Or, had it freed feelings already inside him, to come out, now, that his defenses were down?

The nurse's hand on her shoulder broke through her thoughts. She whispered to Lake that Hawk would probably sleep for six hours or so, then, if all signs were good, he would be moved up to a room. It was imperative the leg wound not open. Lake asked the nurse to write her name down on the list of people allowed to see Hawk when he was moved. The nurse smiled and assured her she would, adding a conciliatory rub to Lake's shoulder.

Lake leaned over Hawk and searched for an unbruised spot on his unshaven cheek to place a heartfelt kiss before she left. How close had she come to losing him? At times like this, the fragility of life made everything so clear. Opened you to truth. Lake's became clear.

The circus in the front lobby barely garnered any of her attention as she made her way slowly out of the hospital, oblivious to everything except thoughts of the man who had uttered what she herself had been afraid, or felt it was too young a thing, to put voice to yet.

Did he even realize what he had said?

She needed sleep. There would be no figuring this out tonight. Just thankfulness they would have time to do so.

BEYOND THE SHADOW

THIRTEEN

The New Ranch Hands

Fran stayed. She insisted on driving River off to school, even though Lake was home before five a.m.

"Get some sleep, hon. I'll get River up and send him in to see you before he leaves for school."

Exhaustion hit Lake like a freight train. She was too tired to say much except, "Thanks, Fran." Then it was down the hall to her bed, where she grabbed the fuzzy pink robe and pulled it over her still fully-dressed self, falling asleep as soon as she hit the pillow.

She woke up briefly when River hugged her, before he left for school. River couldn't have been in a better mood. He knew Hawk was going to be all right and all the people were okay. Good thing he couldn't see Hawk in person right now, he might have a different reaction.

"Fran or I will pick you up after school today. Wait right by the door. And remember what we talked about - about not talking to people you don't know."

"Aw, Lake, I *told* you, I'm six now, I'm *not* a baby. Zach and I are gonna walk home together."

"Zach can ride with us. I'll call his mom. Maybe you guys can get together this evening. I might pick up a pizza to celebrate summer vacation. How would that be?"

"Cool. I'll tell Zach. He can ask his mom."

"Okay you. Have a good last day of first grade bro."

They kissed cheeks and he bounded out the door to Fran's car.

Lake set her phone alarm for ten-thirty and fell back asleep. It seemed like an instant later the strains of *Fur Elise* were floating about her room.

Concern for Hawk's condition this morning, drove her from the bed. In the kitchen, she scrounged up a plastic bag to cover her bandaged foot, then rummaged through the junk drawer, coming up with some green duct-tape left over from one of River's school projects, to secure the top around her calf.

The warm shower rejuvenated and relaxed her, but she forgot how well duct tape stuck.

"Ye-ow." That pretty much cancelled out the relaxed part of it, but, at least she felt ready to rejoin the human race. After dressing quickly, a glass of orange juice and a slice of dry toast, she was out the door. She'd grab a cup of hospital coffee when she got there.

A little after eleven a.m., and the area around the hospital was still a circus—although there were only half as many clowns as the day before. Good news didn't sell as well as bad, she snorted to herself, remembering a different plane crash.

There had certainly been plenty of drama yesterday afternoon. When Hawk was well enough to tell it, she wanted . . . no, she needed . . . to hear the whole story.

Her foot felt better this morning after some time off it—well that, and a couple stiff doses of ibuprofen. It still needed favoring though. Those heel-less slip-ons she'd debated about buying last month were paying for themselves now.

Hawk had been moved to a regular room. A good sign. That meant no complications. She wound through the hallways. There—255. She gave the half-open door a tentative knock and peeked inside.

A nurse was just leaving the room, chuckling to herself and shaking her head. She smiled at Lake as they passed.

"Lake. Come in. Sit." Hawk patted on the right side of his bed, toward the chair. His voice sounded about normal. A little craggy, but a big difference since last night.

"Hi. You seem chipper this morning. How are you doing?" She sat down in the bedside chair.

He frowned and nodded to a spot beside him on the bed. "No. I meant sit *here*." He patted the bed again.

"You are feeling better." Lake gave him a sidelong look. "The "shhhtrong shhtuff" must have worn off." She teased.

"But they said you're not supposed to move around today, and I promised Sam I'd be on my best behavior. He thinks we make each other, in his words, '*lose our cool*.'"

"He does, huh . . . Well, he's right about that." And winked at her. "Did I really say 'shhhtrong shhtuff'?" he shook his head.

"I think it was more like, 'shhhome shhhhtrong . . . shhhtuf'," Lake watched the topaz eyes carefully.

Hawk smiled, but the frown stuck to his brow. "Anything else?"

"What do you mean?"

"Well, I mean . . . did I say anything else? Last night's kind of fuzzy around the edges."

What should she say? *Oh, yeah. There was the part where you said, "Love you . . ."* No way. She was *not* going to let him know he said *that*.

He was searching his fuzzy memory, you could read it on his face. Did he remember?

He'd have to come up with that one again, on his own—when he was off the drugs. She wasn't going to touch that comment with a ten-foot pole.

Lake decided to fade and evade, "It was kind of fuzzy for me too. That four in the morning 'shhhtuff' is for the birds—hard to tell the wakey from the sleepy."

She quickly changed the topic with a tilt of her head and a big sigh, she said, "You had me worried. Seriously. But hey—great job on the rescue, by the way."

Hawk's frown lingered and he hesitated. He searched her face and she thought for a moment he was going to call her out on the evasive tactics, but the change of topic worked.

He beamed. "I have to tell you. That felt so good. Everyone out okay. What a tangled mess. The team really needed that. We've had some disappointments recently." His eyebrows raised and he sighed. "But all good today." He relaxed against the pillows and slipped his hand over hers.

She helped adjust the pillows a bit more, adding, with a wry smile, "Well, be warned. River's looking for a full report—probably several times over."

"He'll have it—several times over, if it makes him happy." He surveyed the room. "As soon as I can get out of this place. They tell me I'm going to be stuck in here till Monday. And that's only if I can find somebody to give me a hand with things at my place for a while."

The offer popped out of her mouth without a second thought. "I can help. I'd be happy to help. Just let me know what you want done. Meals . . . whatever . . . River's on summer vacation after today. He could help too. Feed and water Elle, and Myron. He loves animals. Well, I'd help him with Myron. He hasn't had any experience with horses yet. The book is wrapped up. It's a good time for me and him to do something different anyway . . ."

"Like babysit me?" His mouth stretched in a sideways line. "I dunno— You sure? Your foot—"

"Positive. Your place is beautiful. River would love spending time out there and my foot's a lot better today. By

Sunday, the doctor said I should be able to walk on it pretty much normally."

"Well, then—if you're sure. That'd be great. For me, I mean. I don't know about you two though. You can move in the guest room, or River could stay up in the loft. He'd might get a kick out of that."

"Move . . . in?"

"Well, sure. For the week or whatever. Makes sense. I've got plenty of room. Save gas . . . and time."

Lake hadn't considered this when she offered.

Hawk gave her a hooded look, tinged with a teasing smile. "You have nothing to worry about, Lake. I'm in no shape to ravish you." Pain flickered across the bruised face as he shifted his weight in the bed, "unfortunately, probably not anytime soon." He grimaced, "These ribs—uhh," as he shifted again and forced his lips back into a smile.

"I'm glad your sense of humor wasn't injured in the fall. But you'd better be careful," Lake pointed to a monitor with a spaghetti pot of wires around it, "I think that little machine over there just started to beep a little faster."

Hawk frowned at it. "Huh—nothing important." Then turned back to her. "Well?"

She couldn't refuse him. Didn't want to anyway. "Okay. Why not?"

"Great. Sam has a key to my place in his office. You can get it from him and move your stuff up this weekend if you like." His brows creased. "Check the fridge though. I don't know how well I'm stocked for company." He looked around the room. "They hid my wallet from me." He grumbled.

Lake was worried he was moving too much.

"Hawk. Stop trying to move. Don't worry about a little food. I can manage it for a bit. You can make it up to me." She winked this time, surprising herself.

Hawk flashed a grin back at her and opened his mouth for what she was sure was a devilish response, when a no-nonsense looking nurse came in.

"Time to check your vitals, Mr. Matthews.

Lake scooted off the side of the bed.

"Wonderful." Hawk pulled a face at Lake's move.

"Quiet for a bit," the nurse instructed.

Hawk did as he was told. The nurse checked his BP, temp and everything that had beeped and lit up. "Hmm. Your blood pressure is a little elevated." She gave him an analyzing look. "Are you sick?" The nurse considered him, then Lake, raised her eyebrows and smiled, "Or just healthy?"

Hawk produced a wicked smile, winked at Lake with a chuckle, then winced. "Oooo. It only hurts when I laugh."

Pink from the nurse's comment, Lake was also concerned about Hawk's pain level. She was disturbing his rest.

"I'm going now, so you can rest again."

"No. Lake. Stay."

"The sooner you recuperate, the sooner you can get out of here."

He sighed. "When you put it like that—"

She said her goodbye. From his expression, it wasn't exactly the goodbye he would have wished for, but the nurse was still there, fidgeting with all the hanging, beeping monitors.

"Rest," she said quietly. "River and I will take care of everything. "Lake wiggled her fingers in a little wave and rounded the door out the room.

***

Yes, he should rest so he could get out of there. Lake's reaction to his injury had been weighing on his mind, but she had fared better than he expected. He recognized real concern in her eyes, behind the smiles. Last night's, or he should say her early morning visit remained frustratingly fuzzy. She evidently could handle some anxiety. But how much would she want to? Although he hadn't had any hospitalizations previously, his work with GRRR placed him in a fair amount of 'iffy' situations. Did he have the right to ask her to deal with that? Not to mention her little brother...

Hawk lay there contemplating the pros and cons.

Lake and River staying at his place. The thought gave him a surprising feeling of satisfaction. He mentally patted himself on the back. Even that hurt right now, he smirked. But the spur of the moment plan to have them stay at the ranch, well—sheer genius on his part—though he couldn't be much of a host for a while. Rest. Concentrate on getting out of here. The sooner he could get to the ranch with them, the better. Get his strength back. Let Lake get to know him—and the ranch. Could she fit into his world?

Could he fit into her world?

He was beginning to think it—as in they—could work. Wanted it to work.

Hawk fell asleep with his mind wandering to his veranda and one of the big Adirondack chairs, envisioning Lake sitting in his lap, watching the sunset...

The nurse observed the softly smiling, now sleeping patient when she re-entered the room, satisfied that the elevated temp had been caused by his recent female visitor. Yes, he was injured, but aside from that, he was healthy. She looked back in appreciation at his sleeping figure.

Make that a very healthy man.

***

Between visiting Hawk at the hospital and getting things lined up for their stay at the ranch, the weekend flew by. River went to the hospital with Lake on Sunday, peppering Hawk with questions about the rescues, the downed plane and his injuries. Hawk, good-naturedly, must have answered all his questions—and they were many—at least three times, until Lake reined River in, worried he might be over-tiring the patient patient.

Lake sat quietly during this exchange—listening, learning and enjoying—impressed by Hawk's tolerance with her little brother. Only, it was more than just patience. She could tell he enjoyed River's curiosity by the amber winks he sneaked her way every so often.

This caused a warm feeling, different from anything she had experienced before. Lake hesitated to name it officially, remnants of her previous relationship failure still lingering—though she rarely thought of Jeremy any more. It wasn't fair to Hawk. He was a different kind of man. There was a selfless quality to him. Her heart told her it was safe to love him, but her head still interfered. It was the brain's job after all, to protect the foolish heart.

Lake sighed. Her brain was finding out just how stubborn her heart could be.

***

After much ado with release papers and doctor's instructions Monday morning, Hawk was finally freed from the hospital. Sam and Randy Stewart, aka "Ranger Randy" came to help, much to River's delight.

Lake took the opportunity to pull Sam aside in the lobby. With all that had been going on after the plane crash and Hawk's injury, she still hadn't dealt with the issue of her threatening visitor. It gnawed at her constantly. She had kept River, either in her, or Fran's sight since school had let out. Hawk would need to recuperate a little further before she told him.

"My uninvited visitor told me to keep it, 'Out little secret'."

"Of course, he did. That's what creeps like that count on." They sat in a waiting room and he peppered her with questions about the incident.

She spilled everything she could remember to the sheriff. Unfortunately, it wasn't much. The thug's threat would loom in Lake's mind forever. If anything happened to River—

"I didn't know what to do at first, Sam. Then I cut my foot . . . then the plane . . . and Hawk got hurt . . . I need help." She put her hand on his arm. "I'm in over my head. I'm petrified for River."

Notoriously hard to rattle, Sam's steely expression was new to her. Total sheriff.

"More than likely it was a scare tactic. All the same, I want you to keep your guard up at Hawk's." He considered for a moment. "His ranch might be the best place for River and you until I have a chance to check into this. It'd be hard for someone to sneak up there, with the terrain—and Elle around." He pushed his Stetson back and rubbed his forehead. "It'd be better if Hawk weren't off his feet right now . . ." He adjusted his hat to its normal position and frowned. "But you've got to let him know."

"I know. I was going to, but then . . . this accident . . ."

"He's tough. Tell him."

"Right. I will—just as soon as he gets settled in back at the ranch."

He smiled. "You still might need to tie him down. Hawk's pretty easy going, but something like this'll stir the fire." He shook his head. "After those photos—Colter's still beating that dead horse—now this—I've had my fill of it." He rubbed his forehead again. "And, be sure to tell Hawk you told me about this." His look turned even more serious. "Today, Lake. I'm calling him later tonight."

"Don't worry, I will."

Sam considered her with a frown, "Seriously, today." Then produced one of his million-dollar smiles. "Okay then. I'm sure Hawk's climbing the walls in there. Let's get him home before he drives everyone nuts."

***

Sam drove Hawk in the squad car. The jeep was rougher riding and his truck was too hard to climb into at this point in his recovery.

Sam got a call on his radio as they pulled into Hawk's lane, so he basically dropped him off and tore out.

"Home sweet home." Lake smiled at Hawk as she stood beside him in front of the cabin.

"Amen to that." Hawk agreed wholeheartedly.

She helped him negotiate the steps. River did his part holding the door and carrying Hawk's bag from the hospital. Elle was ecstatic at his return and vocalized some meaningful 'roooww-wows', from which they all got a good chuckle.

"You must be tired. Head for the couch." The color had drained from his face.

He did as Lake suggested. "Yes ma'am."

Lake went over to help with his crutches and get him settled.

"Where do you want these?" She held the crutches.

"That big stack of firewood outside would be good. But, I guess you can set them there for now." He motioned to a spot by the edge of the coffee table, his tone less chipper.

"Sorry. Ribs are . . . uhhh . . ." he puffed, "talking back."

"Remember. I'm your go-fer. Rest your leg . . . and ribs. If you want me to get anything. Holler. Or . . . if . . . I don't know, when you need to re-bandage, but if you need help . . . Let me know." She offered, but frowned a little as she looked at his thigh, the bandaged wound obvious under the dark gray sweats.

Hawk tilted his head and even though pale, managed to produce his dimples at this. The deep voice had a mischievous edge, "Uh . . . Negatory on the bandage help. But thanks, I'll manage. Actually, I'm lucky I'm not singing soprano." He winced at the thought, then his grin widened, obviously enjoying her blush.

"I—I'd be fine." She, answered, a little mad at herself for stammering.

"You think I was talking about you?" he asked, mercifully turning his attention back to patting Elle.

River came running back downstairs from exploring the loft.

"That's so cool. Can I sleep up there? Can I?"

Hawk winked at Lake and gave the okay to River.

River went to Elle, who had plastered herself to Hawk's side ever since he appeared at the door. River managed to coax her to play. It didn't take much coaxing. She was obviously in doggy heaven, now that Hawk was home and she had a new playmate. Her little brother was enamored of the dog, too. They rolled on the floor, River laughing up a storm.

"Can I go outside with her? Does she fetch sticks?" River asked excitedly.

"She's a great fetcher, but you'll have to check with Lake."

"Lake, can I?"

Lake hesitated. She needed to think about that, remembering Sam's advice to be careful. Fortunately, she had time to think about it, since it was past lunchtime. The mention of food was usually a good tactic to distract a growing boy.

"Did you guys realize it is almost one o'clock? Aren't your stomachs growling? How about I make those turkey sandwiches I promised you Hawk?"

"I'm starved. How about you Riv? Hungry?"

"Yeah, I am. Can I give Elle a treat?" He continued petting Elle, who, tail wagging and ears up, ready to continue their play.

Hawk's laugh was indulgent. "Sure. I think she deserves a little something."

Over the weekend, Lake had stocked Hawk's fridge. They ate a lunch of turkey sandwiches with all the fixings and lemonade, around the coffee table with Hawk so he wouldn't have to move from the couch. Conveniently snout level for Elle, she sat comically, watching every bite go to mouths, like she was watching a tennis match, licking her lips every few turns.

"You don't happen to give this dog treats from the table, do you Hawk?" She smiled—already knowing the answer.

"What? Now, would that be proper manners? Hey look. Is that an eagle?" Hawk pointed out the front window.

River and Lake turned toward the front window and were examining the sky, when, the sound of smacking turned their heads back. From the 'little boy' innocent look on this face, Hawk had obviously slipped a bit of turkey from his sandwich to Elle.

They burst out laughing. Then River and Lake followed his lead and gave the lucky dog a treat, too.

"Enough, you big moocher. Now, go lay down."

She obeyed Hawk immediately, taking her favorite place on the couch, while it was free.

The conversation rolled along easily, and after River helped Lake take the dishes to the kitchen, he asked again about taking Elle outside.

"If it's okay with Hawk."

Hawk nodded and suggested they stay in the clearing, just in front of the cabin. He would take a nap while they did. Lake thought the rest and quiet would do him good.

"I'll go with you," added Lake.

It was good to get outside and fill her eyes up with the beautiful Shadowhawk Ranch. She grabbed her camera of course. Elle proved herself to be a great "fetcher". Lake couldn't believe his little arm wasn't tired from all the times he threw the big stick. Then he threw pinecones. Then he sailed his blue Cubs cap out into the meadow.

"River! Not your *Cubs* cap! It'll get all slobbery and chewed up. It's a long way to Wrigley Field to get another." She called out.

"Oh . . . right." He called back, retrieved and brushed it off, then resumed throwing pinecones.

Lake snapped some great pictures of them from her perch on the front porch steps. This was going to be terrific for Riv—for her, too. She enjoyed their lunch. Comfortable. And oh, how she enjoyed that 'little innocent boy' look of Hawk's. He'd make some good-looking kids . . .

Ploink. A pinecone landed in her lap, followed by a big, slobbering mass of panting dog. They were gone in a flash, but River's laughter rang through the meadow.

"All right you." She laughed. It was a challenge to a game of tag, but her foot needed a couple more days of healing, so he was safe from her grasp—for now. Boy and dog frolicked then walked about the meadow. River poked at things on the ground with a stick. Lake could tell he was getting tired. She checked her watch.

"Goodness, Riv. It's four o'clock." Where had the time gone? "We've got to go feed Myron. Oh, and after that Hawk too, I suppose." She kidded.

They hadn't laughed this much in an afternoon since before . . .

They peered in through the front windows. Hawk was still sleeping. River proceeded to the door, but Lake lingered for a moment, watching him through the window, considering her growing attachment to him. *Like a kid at a candy store window* popped into her mind. She hurried to the front door. They tiptoed so as not to awaken Hawk. He woke up a half an hour later.

"Oh, wow." He rubbed his eyes and stretched until his ribs stopped him. "Uhh . . . I was out like a rock."

"It's good for you. You need to heal."

"I'll be back to myself in no time. I've about had it with those things." He kicked at the crutches with his uninjured leg. "It *is* great to be home."

After dinner, River climbed up the steps to the loft and became glued to Animal Planet. Now was her opportunity to tell Hawk about her threatening visitor. She sat on the coffee table next to him. Maybe it would be best to start out on a light note. She lifted her still bandaged foot, resting it on the coffee table.

"Well, we're quite a pair right now. I guess we won't be entering any gunny-sack races in the near future."

He laughed at that. "We'll have to get you to the "Harmony River Round-up," festival this summer, if you're a fan of gunny-sack races. We should be more than healed up and ready for the sack by then." His eyes sparked. "Want to be my partner? There would be a lot of training involved—" His fiery eyes danced with outrageous teasing, punctuated with a wicked, dimpled grin.

"I'll consider it." She couldn't help her own grin from slipping onto her lips, but then narrowed her look and added a serious note, "I'm old fashioned though. I believe certain kinds of training require special licensing..."

They searched each other's eyes for a moment. Hawk broke the silence.

"I realize that about you Lake—we're not so different, you know." He touched her cheek. Her heart started revving up and she frowned as she tried to pull herself back to the mission she set out on. He noticed her hesitation. Concerned, he asked, "Lake, what is it? What's the matter? I'm sorry... I don't mean to rush—"

"No... no. You don't understand. There's something I need to explain."

He tensed. "I feel like I'm about to crash and burn."

"No, not about us. It's something else."

Noticeably relieved, he urged, "What then?"

Lake turned ten shades of serious as she spoke of last Thursday's intruder. If Lake turned ten shades, Hawk turned twenty. His eyes hardened at Colter's new tactic. Anger didn't describe it. A fire was building in him, worthy of his Gaelic namesake.

"I was going to tell you when you got back from picking Riv up from school, but then everything..." She gave a helpless motion with her hands toward his body, from ribs to leg.

Hawk's look softened as he brought his eyes back to Lakes and took her hand.

"Trust me. Colter and his goons won't get near you or River." His hand closed firmly around hers in reassurance as he added, "But I wish you'd told me right away." He took her other hand and pulled her beside him on the couch.

"Trust me. Believe in me . . . I believe in you." His fingers stroked her cheek. "Always."

Lake nodded, unable to speak. This time, she leaned into his kiss—a kiss full of trust and hope.

FOURTEEN

Be Mine

As the result of a life spent outdoors and a strenuous physical fitness regimen, Hawk's recovery progressed at, what the doctor said was a phenomenal pace—much faster than predicted.

Good . . . and bad, Hawk mused, as he watched Lake and River headed to the stable to feed Myron. They needn't stay much longer. The past couple weeks had flown by. He'd soon be up to speed and able to do most things around the ranch, albeit in short episodes. In a couple days, he'd try riding Myron. He'd promise to River to give him his first horseback ride. It would have to be at a very slow walk.

The bruised ribs didn't ache much anymore, and the past few nights he'd been able to lay down to sleep, instead of propped up on pillows. The leg wound had healed nicely. The bruised tendon left him with a slight limp, but it was improving daily, and it was a relief when he tossed the crutches aside.

He'd enjoyed walking around the place with River, laughing, talking, teaching him how ranches work—even a few wilderness skills. He'd never seen a kid so charged—except maybe when he was a kid and fell in love with the place.

River took over the feeding of Elle and Myron—with a little help from Lake. Totally loving the freedom of the ranch, he and Elle faithfully continued the daily search for the supernaturally elusive, Toes. The old raccoon, whose tracks appeared over all sorts of things. continued to be a phantom, allowing only one brief sighting, around dusk two days before. It was the cause of much excitement on River's part and an abundant amount of barking on Elle's.

"Elle's ecstatic she's finally found someone who shows the proper enthusiasm about finding that old raccoon," he'd commented to Lake about the pair.

Though unaware, River was kept under careful watch. Hawk and Sam discussed the situation and decided someone trusted should keep him in their sights until they determined if the threat was real or bluff.

Suzanne made one visit, early on, her excuse—a coffee cake care package. Suz was delighted at seeing Lake and River there—if anyone in Harmony didn't already know they were staying at Shadowhawk, nursing him back to health, they would by now. Never a fan of gossip, Hawk marveled at how satisfied he was at the idea of Suz having passed the news along.

Colter was still pursuing legal action with the trumped-up photos. Hawk spent the better part of one morning muttering at a pile of papers on the old, oak roll-top. He tried, but Lake still wouldn't be budged from testifying as an expert witness.

More of that Scot's stubborn, he supposed and smiled to himself. He'd have to get used to that. He *hoped* he'd have to get used to it. He tried to dissuade her, told her they could find another expert—to no avail. Which, lead him around to the idea of finding an additional expert, or two, anyway, for back up. Perhaps it would take pressure off her—and River, if word got out she wasn't the only expert he had on his side. How many people did Colter think he could threaten?

He sat on the porch watching River and Lake, Elle at their heels, now leading Myron to the corral. Lake left her hair loose today and the breeze tossed it, glinting ebony and chestnut in the morning sun.

The last week and a half had been a real eye-opener. The ranch had always been awe-inspiring, beautiful vistas any which way you turned, but, with Lake's arrival, it came to life with a warmth and glow like never before. Then, there was River. Hawk never knew to miss the energy and joy of having a child around. Now he feared, as he sat and considered his life on this gorgeous June morning, the ranch would forever lack something, a *big* something, when they left.

His eyes drifted to the top step of the porch. He and Lake had taken to sitting there the past few nights, soaking in starlight. Elle even permitted Lake to sit next to Hawk. He closed his eyes to savor the vision. That little scene could get to be habit forming—*real* fast.

How things could change. Not so long ago, he'd sat right there, thinking nothing could surpass the beauty of a starlit Montana night—until he'd seen it reflected in eyes of a certain captivating photographer.

Hawk poked gently at his ribs—barely a twang anymore. He was almost sorry they'd healed so quickly and teetered his grandpa's old chair back against the log wall of the porch. Hawk knew his heart. He was no teenager. He knew what was missing—and he knew when a prayer was being answered.

But Lake had been through so much, he didn't want to ask her to make an emotional decision she would later regret. Could she love him? Would she take the chance?

So, there he sat, teetering, off-balance. Not wanting to rush her, but not wanting to be without her, either.

He was pretty much fine. He'd have to give up the charade soon and let them go home. The show in Denver would be here soon. Maybe they'd stay until he left for that.

A brainstorm. Better yet, he'd ask them to come along. Yeah. That's the ticket. Then, when they got back, he'd sound Lake out.

His thoughts were interrupted by Monica Barnes's dusty blue pickup rattling up the drive. Lake and River waved vigorously as she drove by. Monica had been at her most neighborly since his injury, showing up with so much soup and meatloaf that he had taken to sticking it in the freezer. Thoughtful of her, though. Out here, neighbors still looked out for one another. She'd taken a real liking to Lake and River, too.

Today, from the tinfoil wrapping, it looked like more meatloaf. Hawk inwardly groaned, but thanked her.

"Cup a joe?"

"Don't mind if I do . . . No. Don't get up. I'll take this in and grab a cup. Be right back."

She appeared a couple minutes later with a steaming mug of coffee and a frown. "Looks like you're out of all of that coffee cake Suzanne brought. I'll have to make you another one." Still tough at sixty, she nodded as she sat down in a chair.

"Monica . . . You've done too much already. Don't go to any more trouble. Really."

"No trouble." She reached over and patted his knee. "No trouble at all. It's what neighbors do."

They sat for a few minutes, watching Lake and River go about the chores. Then, Hawk felt Monica's keen eyes on him.

Her grey eyes twinkled at him. "Well, what do you know? Finally." She laughed softly. "Fond of her, aren't you? Could get used to having her around here, I'd be willin' ta bet."

He smiled broadly—he couldn't help it. "More than pretty fond. Yeah." He continued to watch Lake. "That obvious, huh?"

"She the one?" Monica's eyes sparkled with the question.

"Cut to the chase as always, Monica. He might as well be frank. "You know . . . I think she just may be." He turned to her. "Keep that under your hat for now."

"Of course." Smiling like a Cheshire cat, she turned back to Lake and River. "The little boy's a cute one too . . . kinda reminds me . . ." Her voice trailed off in a memory.

"I'm gettin' hungry, how about you?" Hawk prompted, mainly to pull her away from where she seemed headed.

Lake and River ambled back from the barn. After a little discussion, Monica insisted on showing Lake how to make Suzanne's spicy, wake-you-up, "Cinn-a-morn" coffee cake. Monica explained she'd finagled the secret recipe out of Suzanne in exchange for her own, "Wildberry Pie" recipe.

Monica and Lake went to the kitchen while Hawk and River headed for the living room. Elle raced ahead for her spot on the couch.

"You have cinnamon?" Monica asked as she opened cabinets.

"The spices are in here." Lake pulled open a narrow vertical drawer, stocked with a good assortment of spices and herbs. She inhaled the pleasant mixture of aromas it released.

"Getting to know your way around the place pretty well, I see." Monica commented with raised eyebrows and a knowing smile.

Lake's blush answered for her.

After gathering all the ingredients, the hunt for a cake pan was on, to no avail. Hawk was sure he kept one in the cabinet beside the oven, and came over to help look. After much clanking, he gave up admitting he hadn't attempted to bake a cake for so long, it was hard telling.

"It's all right. I've got one at my place. I'll pop over and get it. Be back before you know it."

"No, Monica. Don't go to that much trouble. We can have scrambled eggs and toast for breakfast." Lake insisted.

"No . . . I insist. I promised to show you how to make Suzanne's coffee cake. I never break a promise. I'll be right back."

Hawk shook his head at Lake's look. He knew better than to argue with Monica.

"You want to ride along?" Monica asked River. "Give you two a little alone time, huh?" she asked with a chuckle and wink at Hawk.

"Can I Lake? Can I?" River pleaded.

Lake looked to Hawk. "It's only a couple of miles to Monica's, isn't it? They should be back soon?"

"Fifteen minutes," Hawk answered.

"I'm sure you two will put the time to good use." The older woman's eyes twinkled.

River was waiting at the door. "Can I, Lake? Can I?"

Lake gave in to his dancing pleading. "Okay. *Okay.*" Lake's tone turned serious. "You can go, but stay right with Monica." He was already out the door as she called after him to behave himself.

"I will. Promise."

He scrambled into the truck and they were off.

Lake, arms on hips, shaking her head and chuckling softly, watched them go down the drive. Hawk came up behind her then and gently pulled her back against his chest. He wrapped his arms around her resting his cheek on the top of her head. "Umm . . . Oh, yeah, Wildcat, I've been wanting to do this all morning." He inhaled the clean, appealing scent of her s dark hair and nuzzled her ear, flipping her stomach and sending goosebumps clear down to her toes.

"Ummm . . . Careful *Fire-man* . . . your ribs . . ." She hesitated before relaxing back against him.

"Oh yeah—about the ribs. The good news is," he turned her in his arms to face him, "we can do this." He encompassed her in a firm hug. "The bad news, for me anyway, is that I can manage things around here again." Guilty dimples appeared as he held her and brushed her hair back from her face.

"I thought you were hamming it up a bit lately." Lake's eyes danced at Hawk's frown at being called out on his acting ability. "But, you know, I feel the same way," she looked up at him. "I—"

He effectively ended her declaration with a kiss. The rest of their admissions took a couple of minutes and were completely wordless, leaving Lake much more breathless than words ever could have. Hawk pulled back with a satisfied smile.

She reached up and traced the dimple in his cheek.

"Something I've been wanted to do all morning."

"We were supposed to put the time to good use." Then, brushing a kiss across the tip of her nose, told her of his idea about them joining him for the Denver show.

Lake didn't try to hide her enthusiasm. They discussed plans as they walked, hand in hand, down to the stream . . . and back. Lake was so happy; it took a few minutes for her to float back down to earth.

"What time is it?" she asked as they stepped onto the front porch steps.

"Ten forty-five." He frowned and tapped absently at the watch face, then turned and peered down the lane. "Huh. It was what. . . a couple minutes to ten when they left?"

Lake's gaze followed his, toward the main road. "Oh, you know River. I'm sure he's asked her a thousand questions by now and had to snoop all over her place." She couldn't hide the note of anxiety that crept into her voice by the end of the sentence.

"You're right. Just the same, let's give them a quick call."

Did Hawk want to ease her mind . . . or his own?

Relief, everything was fine. According to Monica, Lake's assumption about River had been correct. He was in the bathroom just then, but he'd persuaded her to give him a tour around her house and yard. Lake laughed and nodded her head knowingly when Hawk relayed Monica's side of the conversation.

"They should be headed back shortly." He put his arms back around her. "Now, where were we?"

"We'll be cooking lunch instead of breakfast." She quipped. "But that's okay. We can always warm up some meatloaf." She giggled at Hawk's groan. "And have coffee cake for dessert."

His arms went around her and her lifted her off the porch floor and swung her in a circle half-laughing, half-groaning at her teasing about the prospect of eating more meatloaf, before setting her back down.

"It's great having you here—and River, too."

The smiling words spoken softly into her lips came just before the kiss. A sigh later, they parted.

Lake cleared her throat and stepped back, trying to steer the conversation to a topic that would keep them out of each other's arms for a few minutes. She needed to catch her breath—and keep her senses about her.

"What's your next project?" She looked toward the studio.

He grinned at her maneuver, and she was sure he had read her thoughts.

"I do have an idea I'm pursuing—in the planning stages, you understand," he smiled warmly and winked. It was Lake's turn to blush a little.

He grabbed her hand and chuckled, "C'mon. Let's walk down to the studio."

As they walked, Hawk asked about her next project, too. He loved the *Snowshine on Shadow* idea and expressed amazement at the photos he'd seen on her camera. It was food for the soul, getting jazzed by one another's interest and encouragement—almost as good as being in the zone, during the actual creative process.

Lost in this warm cloud of emotion, Lake was a more than a little shocked when her peripheral vision caught the time on the wall clock in the studio.

"Twenty after eleven!?" A darkness crept over her mood. "I probably shouldn't have let River go with Monica. I told him to behave himself. He's probably driving her crazy with questions by now." Lake stepped back from Hawk and pulled out her phone. "What's Monica's number?"

When there was no answer, Lake's alarm bells blared—more so at Hawk's expression. He tried calling also and moved outside toward his truck. Still no answer.

"Elle!" he yelled sharply, "C'mon girl. Let's go for a ride." Then to Lake, "Nice morning for a drive. Let's take a drive over and see what's keeping them." Elle was already at the truck, waiting to hop in.

"Do you think everything's all right?" Lake hurried to keep up with his stride—there was barely a trace of a limp left from his injury.

"More than likely. Let's be on the safe side."

Not much was said on the ride over. Lake repeatedly dialed Monica's number—still no answer. No point in leaving another voicemail. What was going on? What could be keeping them? Didn't Monica realize they would be worried? She would have to bite her tongue when she talked to Monica.

A scary question flooded Lake's mind. Could someone have followed them? Monica's place was so close, and everything had been so quiet lately, she'd thought a fifteen-minute trip with an adult, would be all right.

Shake it off, she told herself. She was probably just being paranoid.

As if he understood, Hawk reached a hand over and rubbed her knee, just for a moment. "It'll be okay. We'll figure this out. They probably got sidetracked, you know River. And sometimes, the way this terrain runs, cell phones can be pretty iffy."

"The call went to voice mail, Hawk. It made the connection," she said flatly.

His only response—another reassuring rub to her knee.

Lake noticed their increased speed. Too much on these roads and it'd be a one-way thrill ride to the bottom of the valley. Hawk was pushing the envelope as much as he dared.

After ten minutes that seemed like an eternity, the Barnes place came into view. Lake jumped out of truck the before it skidded completely to a stop. Elle was hot on her heels as she raced up the front porch and rapped on the door.

"River. River!" Lake's dread grew. "River? Monica?"

Nothing.

Hawk went to the far side of the porch, leaned over the railing, and peered around back.

"Her truck's out back. Try the door."

Unlocked.

"River? Monica?" Hawk hollered into the house as they searched the first floor.

With a desperate, sinking feeling, she grabbed Hawk's arm. "Where are they?"

She let go his arm and spun round in distress, hands to her head. "I must have been crazy, letting him go. What was I thinking?"

Hawk put an arm behind her and moved them toward the door at the rear of the kitchen. "Let's look out back," he said, dialing his phone at the same time. "Sam. Thank God. Listen—we have a problem up here at the Barnes's place—"

Lake ran into the backyard. Nothing. She headed for the barn, Hawk a short distance behind. She was aware of his ongoing conversation with Sam as they searched the barn. Hawk said something about calling the team.

"They're not here, Hawk. Oh, God, please . . ." Lake prayed and doubled forward trying not to be sick. Hands on her knees and she closed her eyes and tried to breathe. Think of what to do next.

Hawk rubbed a hand over his jaw and looked around. "Hopefully, he's just wandered off and is still nearby." They walked outside the barn into the yard where Elle attracted their attention. She ran off barking and was now running back to them from the direction of the lane which they drove in on . . . with something in her mouth.

Lake froze at the sight. Hawk took River's blue Cubs cap from Elle's mouth. With a cry, she grabbed the cap from him and sank to her knees.

"What could have happened—that he deserted his Cubs cap?"

Hawk, now grim-faced, helped her up and took her to a bench outside the barn. He sat her down and told her to wait. "We'll figure it out," he said, but his voice was muffled by the rushing sound in her head. He walked a distance away, on his phone again. She slumped forward, arms and head on knees. All she could manage at that moment, was a continuation of her *God, please, God, please*, mental prayer-chant.

A small plane passed overhead. "GRRR." Hawk told Lake. "Mike, one of our pilots happened to be at the airport. Got her right up. Said he'd take a look around. Sam and the guys are on their way. He's bringing Slug. We'll get both dogs working."

They were watching the plane fly overhead, when, out of the trees at the side of her place stumbled a disheveled Monica Barnes.

"Monica!" He shouted.

Their eyes searched the hill behind her for River as they ran to her. She had a bump the size of a goose-egg on her forehead. Hawk picked her up. Lake ran a few feet past them, trying to spot River.

"Monica. What happened? Where's River? Monica?"

"I . . . a . . ." Was all she managed to get out.

"I'm taking her inside. Be right back. Look around this area, but don't go very far in."

Lake, with Elle by her side, nodded and started searching and calling for River on the thickly forested hill. Hawk was back before she knew it.

"What happened? Did she say what happened?" Lake asked desperately.

"All she said was she told River he could wait on the porch while she got the pan from the kitchen and then a couple minutes later, she went out and he was gone."

"He was gone? Just like that? He was *gone*?!" She gave an exasperated sigh. "That's *not River*, Hawk. He wouldn't do that. What was she doing out here—on this hillside? Why didn't she call us?"

"She said she was looking for him and fell. Hit her head." He frowned and looked at the ground around them. "Dropped her phone someplace—"

Lake looked at him, desperation in her eyes. "Wha—what now?"

His thumb rubbed at the blue cap he'd taken back from her. He considered. "We've got his cap. It has his scent. We'll get Elle looking for him. And Sam and the some of the guys should be here in a few minutes. Sam's bringing Slug. That bloodhound's got an even better nose than Elle." He pulled her in for a reassuring hug. "We'll find him."

Taking River's cap, he squatted in front of the dog, instructing her to, "Find him. Yeah, you know River . . . that's a girl . . . get a good whiff. Find River. Find River . . . Go. Find."

With one, sharp bark, Elle ran down the hill into the yard and out along the lane. Then, she began running back and forth from Monica's porch to a spot near the point on the lane where she picked up his cap. Hawk and Lake came down the hillside and stood in the drive a little way away from her.

"Find him Elle. Find River."

Elle barked at him and ran the same pattern again. Hawk rubbed the dark growth on his jaw line, frowning at the dog.

"What does that mean? Hawk?" She tugged at his bicep. "Why is she just running back and forth there? Hawk! Is she confused? Hawk?"

"No—I don't think so. That's where she finds his scent." He walked the path of the lane toward the main road and back, examining the ground.

Lake was busy trying to decipher his expression when flashing blue and red lights began dancing across his face. She looked toward the road as the sheriff's car and a half-dozen assorted vehicles came up the lane.

Hawk waved them to stay back, away from the area Elle was designating. Sam, his big bloodhound Slug, and the rest of the guys made their way to Hawk.

Sam and Hawk looked at Elle and then each other.

"That's it? That's what she's got?" Sam's frown matched Hawk's.

"Yeah." Hawk shot a look at Sam. Lake knew it wasn't good. "Let's see what Slug can come up with."

Sam's dog did about the same thing, ending up not more than a foot away from where Elle stopped. Then, Slug woofed and ran a few feet further down the lane toward the trucks and the main road.

"Oh, dear God." Lake whispered. "Does that mean what I think?"

Any reassurance offered by Hawk's arm over her shoulders was nullified by his grim look and tone of voice when he'd addressed Sam.

"You need to bring Colter in. Now."

"I've got Pat and Cal on that. But, word is he's been in Kalispell all morning. We're checking things out."

"Yeah? What about that goon who paid Lake a visit?" He narrowed his look to Sam. "What about that guy?"

"That guy is Eddy Blake—an associate of Colter's. Petty thief. Did time for assault down in Colorado a few years back." He stared back at Hawk. "I have been on it, Hawk. But—from intimidation to actual kidnapping?" Sam shook his head. "It doesn't make sense for Colter. It's an escalation I wouldn't think he'd want to chance." Sam appraised the scene.

"You think he's responsible for this?" Lake wrapped her arms around herself, tormented. "I should have never let River go. It's my fault. Why did I ever—?"

"Lake. Stop. Stop," Hawk repeated and held her, rubbing her arms. "That's no good now. I thought it'd be okay too—remember? We've got to concentrate on finding River." He looked around. "Why don't you go in the house. See how Monica's doing. Let us—we're going to organize a search. We'll figure out what to do next."

Numb with worry, she nodded and stumbled off toward the house, leaving the lights and commotion going on behind her. What else could she do? She'd looked everywhere nearby.

She sat down heavily on the top porch step and, elbows on knees and face in hands, she concentrated. "Shepherd ... find our lamb. Find our lost lamb. Help us find River," Lake whispered the simple prayer over and over.

She didn't know quite how long she sat there, but when she looked up, Hawk was there, taking her by the shoulders, urging her the rest of the way into the house. She sat down in the living room.

Monica held a cool pack on her forehead. The EMT that examined her said it didn't appear to be anything serious—just a significant bump. Monica smiled and said she'd be fine.

She'd be fine. Fine?! How could she be *fine*? River was out there ... somewhere.

Lake sat in silence with Monica, the activity outside the only noise. Lake's gaze locked on a patch of light on the living room wall flashing blue, then red, then blue, then red, over and over and over and over ...

BEYOND THE SHADOW

FIFTEEN

Into the Light

A plan was quickly devised. They would search the area, just in case the dogs had missed anything. It was unlikely, but everyone wanted to make sure they covered all the bases. Word came, via a call from Pat, that he and Cal had located Eddy Blake in a Kalispell bar and were bringing him in for questioning. Sam sped off to town to meet them, but left Slug to help with the search. Hawk checked on Lake and Monica, then headed out onto the surrounding hillsides with the others, leaving the place, disturbingly quiet.

Lake renewed her prayers and tried to keep her mind off what River must be feeling . . . or thinking . . . if he was scared . . . or hurt.

Monica seemed to be feeling better. Doing a lot better than Lake. She insisted on making tea for them while they waited. Lake couldn't help thinking what a tough old bird she was. She supposed she had to be, living out here by herself all these years. All that had happened to her in her life. Losing her husband, then Joey.

Monica place two cups of chamomile tea on the coffee table in front of them.

"Here, drink this. It will comfort." Monica pushed the teacup a little closer to Lake.

Lake tried a smile, but it died halfway to her lips.

"I know exactly how you're feeling Lake . . . Believe me . . . Hawk sure looked sick. He looked as if he his own son was lost. He really cares for that boy, I can tell . . ."

If she was trying to comfort her, Lake thought, it wasn't the best choice of words.

They sat and sipped the tea . . . and waited . . . and waited. All kinds of guilt washed over Lake. She should be out there. Next time Hawk called, she would insist on it.

The light was fading. It would be dark soon. The thought of River out there, alone in the dark . . . Her thoughts spun.

Monica got up off the couch. "Do you need some fresh air? Want to come out on the porch for a while? I sat on the porch a lot while they looked for Joey."

Again . . . *not helping* . . . She wished Monica would keep her reflections of the past to herself. After all, that event had a bad outcome.

"No. Thanks. I just want to sit here . . . maybe in a few minutes."

"The fresh air would do you good. I wish Hawk would come back down from the hill. He should really be here waiting with you," she said and went out the front door and the sound of her footsteps receded in the distance, down the boards of the porch.

When would they hear anything? The last bit of light was fading. Aside from a call a couple hours ago to check on her—and insisting for Lake to stay put, she hadn't heard anything more from Hawk. Or Sam. Or anyone.

A noise brought her thoughts back. Lake grabbed for her phone . . . But her phone wasn't ringing . . . *What in the* . . . She looked around . . . the ringing continued, slightly muffled, but it was definitely a phone . . . Lake followed the noise to a denim jacket hanging on the hall tree by the door. It sounded like a phone. She reached in the pocket. A phone? Monica had dropped hers in the trees . . . Whose was this? Wasn't this the jacket Monica was wearing?

Lake decided to find out. "Hello?"

"Lake? Lake, is that you?" It was Hawk's voice. Hawk's surprised voice. "Where are you? I told you to stay in the house and wait. It's getting dark. You can't be out wandering—"

Lake interrupted him. "I *am* in the house . . . in Monica's living room. This phone was in . . . her jacket pocket, here by the door. Whose phone is this? Who did you call?"

There was an extended silence.

"I called Monica's number. I thought I'd see if I could locate her phone on the hillside. See where she'd been."

"Wha . . . that doesn't make any sense. She lost her phone in the trees . . . on the hillside. She said so. This was . . . in a pocket of her jacket." Lake told him, confused.

"Yeah—uh—evidently, she didn't," he said, his tone flat. Then, with a sudden urgency to his voice, "Lake. Listen to me. Where's Monica?"

"Getting some air, out on the porch," she answered, her confusion growing.

"Lake, I'm on my way down. Listen, something's not right here. My keys are in my truck. Drive it to the main road. Don't tell her about the phone. Say you're going to talk to Sam. Just leave. I'll meet you on the road. Go—now!"

Confused, Lake slipped the phone in her pocket and turned to do as Hawk requested—just in time to catch a glimpse of a piece of firewood coming at her head. Lake ducked—but not in time. It caught her on the side of the face, sending her sprawling across the hardwood floor.

"Not exactly the way it was supposed to turn out, but still—"

Dazed, Lake touched the side of her head. Wet. Her fingers—red. Blood. She blinked hard, trying to make sense. On hands and knees, she skidded toward the side of the room, away from Monica.

"Wha . . . what are you doing? Why? I . . . I don't underst—"

"I was beginning to think I'd never get to make him pay for my Joey. My sweet boy. It was all Hawk's fault—all his fault. I waited . . . thought he'd never get married ... have a son of his own. But then you came along—with that child. Worked out pretty well . . . Hawk fell for both of you." She croaked. "Now Hawk Matthews will get the payback he deserves." Monica's head tilted crookedly at Lake. "Except, you weren't supposed to find out—were supposed to think Colter made him disappear—and I could've just watched it all happen." She squinted. "Now, what to do—with you?"

Intent on getting out of the cabin, Lake scrambled to her feet and toward the door, but not in time. Monica reached up and grabbed her rifle from the wall rack.

"Whoa . . . No you don't . . ." She looked around. "Let's go for a ride."

"I'm not going anywhere with you," Lake answered firmly.

The sound of booted footsteps running up the porch steps turned their attention to the door. Monica turned the rifle and motioned Lake to the door. "Outside."

"Now! Everybody . . . Out . . . Out in the yard," Monica ordered. "This is Matthews's payback. No need for all of you to get hurt—but don't think I won't."

Hawk winced at the sight of the blood on Lake's face and started toward her.

"Get away from her. Throw your keys over here. I *will* shoot *you*. I don't want to, but I will if I have to. You should have *years* of suffering . . . but don't think I won't end you—or maybe just a kneecap for now. Now *move*!"

In the yard, she kept the rifle trained on them and ordered. "Okay boys, empty your pockets. Real slow. I can shoot an eyelash off a grizzly . . . Ask Hawk . . . Nothing funny, now."

The guys looked to Hawk and at his nod, emptied their pockets on the ground. Monica ordered them to backup. After she gathered up the keys, she headed for Hawk's truck. She kept the gun trained on them as she maneuvered herself into the truck.

"Lay flat on the ground." She shot a round into the dirt when the dogs headed in her direction. They yipped at the gravel sprayed their way and stopped.

"Stay Elle. Stay Slug. Monica . . . Tell us . . . Where's River? *Monica* . . . Take *me* with you. Shoot me right now—either way—just don't take revenge on an innocent kid." Hawk tried to convince her.

"Innocent? My Joey was innocent. I could have shot you years ago. Too easy. Now . . . all of you . . . down . . . the rest of the way. You'll never find him. An eye for an eye. That's the way."

They all laid on the ground.

"Now you'll suffer like you deserve. Like I suffered." She spat the words and shot another round into the dirt beside them, then peeled out, racing down the lane in Hawk's truck.

***

As soon as the truck started moving, they were up and scrambling to find any keys she'd missed in the dirt, trying to reorganize. Not more than a minute later, the sound of a siren wafted in their direction.

"That's Sam... Must've caught sight of Monica." Hawk stated with a frown as they all turned in the direction of the sound. Another siren now.

"Not far... mile? What'd ya think?" asked Randy.

"I'd say," answered Hawk.

Then—the sound of screeching and crashing.

"*Anyone* have keys?" Hawk asked desperately.

"I think there's still a spare under my fender," from Randy, followed by a "Got it."

Hawk, Lake and Randy loaded into the big, black four by four and raced the quarter mile down to the main road. They rounded the bend to the sight of Sam and two deputies looking down into the ravine. From the looks of the brush, it was obvious someone had gone over the side.

Monica couldn't have gone off road in a worse spot. They located her body a few minutes later. She had been thrown from the truck about halfway down.

Sam explained what they had gathered in town. "Eddy Blake spilled everything when threatened with arrest. Strictly a small-time hood—didn't want to go down for kidnapping. Told us Colter had paid him to scare Lake. Colter bragged to him that he was, "egging the old Barnes woman on"—about Joey's death being Hawk's fault. Colter thought he could get her on his side—put more pressure on Hawk to sell out. I was on my way back up here to question Monica when she comes flying around the corner in Hawk's truck." He shook his head. "About ran me off the edge."

**

Lake stood beside Sam's Explorer and clung to Hawk. It was dark now and their best chance at finding River had just gone over the side of the mountain.

Amid the eerie scene, lit by flashing emergency lights and floodlights pointed off down the hill, Hawk took hold of Lake's shoulders and pushed her gently back from him. The expression on his face was one Lake had never seen before—grim in the strange light. It matched his tone.

His hands dropped from her shoulders. He touched the blood on the side of her face. Voice like gravel, shoulders slumped, he turned his head away, rubbing a hand over his eyes. "I'm sorry . . . so sorry . . . What I've brought down on you and River . . . didn't deserve this . . . *any* of this . . . *God . . . Why?* His face turned upward, but his eyes remained closed, when they met hers again, his torment was evident.

Lake felt his pain . . . and hers . . . and River's—wherever he was. Pain, but pain that was not of Hawk's doing. It was her turn to take his shoulders.

"Hawk," she pleaded. "Hawk. Listen to me . . . None of this is your fault . . . it's all on Monica . . . not you. Her choices—all her." Lake squeezed his arms—the tears running freely down her cheeks. "You helped me—showed me—there was hope." She swallowed hard. "I believe in you. You can find River." Her grip on his arms tightened.

"Go. Do what you do. What you've trained to do. You know how to do this Hawk."

Lake couldn't prevent the catch in her voice as she ended her plea. "I need you in my future . . . need both of you in my future."

***

Hawk rubbed an arm across his face and pulled Lake to him again. He laid his cheek across the top of her head for the briefest of moments, then, set her back from him.

He wiped at the tear stains on her cheeks.

"I love you." He kissed the top of her head and, with renewed resolve, said, "We've got work to do."

He rested her back against the car and headed back to the GRRR group.

"What are we missing guys?" Hawk asked the group. "The dogs clearly showed River's scent at the lane . . ."

With the words, the seed of an idea began to germinate.

"Monica had a little over an hour. She couldn't have gone far. She wanted revenge . . ."

He rubbed his head. Looked to Sam.

"Revenge," Sam echoed.

"The mine." they said simultaneously.

"Let's get over there," Hawk added.

"But the dogs—they indicated the road," Cal interjected.

"A couple of our trucks were parked across the old track that leads to the mine. Could we have misinterpreted?" Randy questioned.

"Let's go." Hawk said.

Sure enough, when the dogs followed the scent further, past all vehicles, the trail veered off in the direction of the old mine, not the highway.

"We were so sure it was Colter or his goon—we assumed they were headed for the highway." Sam shook his head.

They regrouped and geared up for the mine. The rest of the guys, their keys still somewhere down the ravine with Hawk's wrecked truck, loaded into the back of Randy's pickup and they headed for the mine.

After a ten-minute drive on the washed-out, abandoned road they unloaded the dogs—who immediately ran for the mine. They circled—barking, waiting for more orders—when told to stay by the entrance.

"It's dangerous in there. I can't believe she chanced it," said Sam.

"I'll go. I can't believe any of this. But in the state of mind—or out of mind—Monica was in, I don't think she was worried much about that," Hawk added.

"You sure you're okay for this?" Sam frowned.

"I'm fine." Hawk lied, burying the pain that had flared up when he and Lake searched the hillside. Nothing was going to stop him now, from going in that nightmare of a death-trap he'd been avoiding all these years.

Hawk gave the agitated Elle a sharp "Quiet!" and led her into the mine. Slow going—didn't want the whole place coming down on them.

"River! Can you hear me? River!" He called the boy's name every so often, but got nothing except a showering of powder from the ceiling. One good sneeze could bring the place down, but there was no avoiding it. He had to call. He and Elle listened for any response. Nothing.

About ten minutes in, Elle got excited.

"Yeah, that's it Elle. Find him girl. Find River." Hawk spoke as loud as he dared, the amount of powder showering from overhead was becoming more and more alarming. Heart hammering, his hopes skyrocketed at the dog's excitement.

The dog led a few feet off the main trunk into in a side chamber, where the beam of his flashlight caught the object of her excitement.

A black tennis shoe with red stripes. River's. He'd seen the boy wear them many times. Hawk frowned and shined his light around the chamber. There were footprints—looked to be about the size of a woman's boot.

But, no child's tracks? A lone tennis shoe? The realization hit him. *Why—the warped, old hag.*

Timbers above creaked and moaned as Elle barked a warning.

***

The distant rumbling first silenced, then set the group outside the mine to yelling. "Back up!" and "Get back!" filled the air as the group scrambled for safety.

Lump in throat, and after a yank from Sam Lake ran too—.

A dirty cloud belched from the mouth of the mine. It blocked everything for a few moments. The dusky powder choked out Lake's desperate cry. "Hawk! River!"

***

Seconds later came the bark, then a man and dog emerged at full run from the cloud, just ahead of a ground rattling *whump* and an even bigger cloud that covered them all.

Lake coughed and stumbled toward Hawk, thankful he was alive, eyes searching his arms for River. The stunned realization hit—no River. She dropped hard to her knees—all her hope crushed as the collapsed mine.

Hawk struggled to control a fit of coughing from the dust and his tender ribs. "Sam." More coughing. "Randy. Cal. Work the hillsides—both sides of the mine." He straightened up, fighting the coughing, brushing himself off. He peered off into the darkness. "She left him out here someplace, I'm sure of it. All I could find inside were her footprints and one of his tennis shoes. More coughing. "I think she meant to throw the dogs off—wanted me to go deeper in there. But I spotted a couple of woman-sized boot prints, just before—" He coughed again.

A somber Sam considered the collapsed mine. "Sure hope you're right." he added quietly.

Hawk grabbed Lake's hand and pulled her to her feet, his only word, "Pray."

Hawk, Elle and the other men fanned out into the darkness.

Pat bandaged the scrape on her face and made a small fire. They sat and waited, listening to the searchers calls for River become fainter as they worked their way farther out.

Please protect River . . . Be beside him —let him enjoy this warmth soon.

Twenty minutes of angst and fervent prayer later, Pat's radio crackled to life. It was Cal.

"We . . ." the radio crackled and buzzed.

"We—what?" Lake jumped to her feet, emotions of hope and fear mixing together.

The crackling finally cleared.

"We've got him! We found the boy."

Lake grabbed Pat's arm in anticipation. "Thank God! Is he all right?"

"What's his condition? Is he all right?" Pat asked.

"Yes. Cold. Gonna need warming up. Back in fifteen."

Lake choked back joyful tears and thought a fervent prayer of thanks. Pat gave a whoop of celebration which was followed by the others. Hugs were exchanged all around. They made cocoa in the big, yellow GRRR truck and waited impatiently, expressing astonishment at the events of the day.

Fifteen minutes later, a commotion at the tree line signaled Hawk's emergence into the circle of flashing lights, carrying River, the little boy bundled in Hawk's GRRR jacket. Hawk's teeth shone white through all the mine dust covering him as he beamed at Lake.

She'd never seen a more wonderful sight than the two people she loved most in the world emerging from those trees with the big dog at Hawk's side. She stumbled over the dark, rock-strewn ground to get to them. Once there, she hugged River tightly, burying her face, tears and kisses on the top of his mussed hair.

River's little boy voice sounded weak and confused, but relieved. "Monica said we were going to meet you guys out there. That you decided for us to have a picnic," he told Lake. "I'm sorry. She was lying, wasn't she? She took my shoe and ran away from me. And I lost my cap . . . but I stayed . . . I didn't wander . . . Hawk said not to wander, if you're ever lost . . . I stuffed grass in my jacket too, to keep warmer, just like Hawk said . . . but I'm still kinda cold . . .

"We've got hot cocoa sweetie, and, don't worry, we found your Cub's cap." Taking River from Hawk's arms, she dropped to her knees in front of the little boy. Gathering him to her with the biggest of bear hugs, she planted kisses on the top of his head—moves that normally would have drawn instant objection in public—but not tonight.

"Love you," River said.

"Love you more," Lake answered and renewed her hug to him as she lifted her gaze to the face of the man she had tried so hard to hate, but had instead come to cherish.

"I'll always love you."

Hawk's answering smile nearly outshone the campfire. He hoisted River onto his back and tucked Lake to his side. Then, the three, entwined in a kind of walking embrace,

BEYOND THE SHADOW

with Elle dancing around them, made their way toward light and warmth—and the promise of their future.

ABOUT THE AUTHOR

JULEE BAKER writes and paints from her home in South Dakota, where wide-open spaces and starry skies that spill out into forever, give her room to wander and dream big. When not at her keyboard or easel, you might find her attempting to turn her urban landscape into a forest.

Author's note: I hope you enjoyed Hawk and Lake's story. Don't you think Sheriff Sam deserves his own book? It's up next in the ABOVE & BEYOND series.

Reviews, no matter how brief, are always appreciated!

Thanks for reading!

CPSIA information can be obtained
at www.ICGtesting.com
Printed in the USA
LVHW091257180819
628045LV00002B/158/P